Midnight Traveller

Midnight Traveller

Pat Coleman

Scripture Union
130 City Road, London EC1V 2NJ

By the same author:
Race the Wind (Tiger Book)

First published 1988

ISBN 0 86201 475 1

Phototypeset by Input Typesetting Ltd., London
Printed and bound in Great Britain by Cox and Wyman Ltd., Reading

1

'Oi, horse! Over here! See what I've got for you,' Joe 'Fingers' O'Brien called loud and clear. At the same time he held out the windfall apple that he had found in the orchard.

The horse in the paddock had a coat which was the warm colour of honey and its long flowing mane had the glint of shining silver. It was the most beautiful living creature that Joe had ever seen, and he had stared at it for ages, awestruck, before offering it the treat.

Joe advanced a step and then another, moving carefully so that the magnificent animal should not be frightened away. 'Horses are supposed to like apples, and this is a good 'un. No worm holes.'

The horse tossed its head, and the mane of soft silken strands rippled along its curved neck. It snorted and Joe smiled. 'I guess that means you know I'm here, so come on, take it,' he coaxed as he reached its side.

The horse looked him up and down with soft dark eyes. Its upper lip slowly curled, and what Joe could only call an insulting sneer appeared on its velvety mouth.

'Hey, come off it!' he protested in surprise.

The horse moved away and from the corner of his eye Joe caught the swift movement of its nearest hind leg. Instinctively he dived to one side, and an iron-shod hoof shot by, barely missing his skinny rump.

Joe rolled over and over in the long grass, his heart thudding, until he met the solid reassurance of a fence post. He got up, dusted himself off and watched dumbfounded as the horse pranced to the other side of the paddock, turned to give him a final look of withering scorn and went back to grazing.

'So much for making friends,' Joe muttered in disappointment. He was still clutching the apple so he rubbed it along his baggy jeans and took it with him over the fence and up into a crotch of the nearest tree.

This was a weird place, Joe decided, as he munched and watched the splendid creature from afar. For the hundredth time since his arrival at Windrush Farm on the previous day, he wished that he were back in his council flat in his beloved city with its smoke, grimy buildings, traffic and people: short and tall people, people with problems, some who laughed, but all of them fascinating. The countryside was going to bore him silly, and his social worker had been a wimp to send him here.

Joe looked eight years old and was actually ten. He was small and delicately built with thin bones, brown eyes and a cap of curling tangled black hair, but he was tough as old boots. He wore a checked cotton shirt, a worn leather belt and jeans. In his shirt pocket he carried a gold box of stale cigarettes. He didn't like to smoke, it made him feel sick, but a cool image was important in the neighbourhood where he came from.

Apple eaten, he tossed away the core and took a ping-pong ball from his pocket. He practised rolling it through his long agile fingers, slipping it in and out, over and under. His friends had not nicknamed him 'Fingers' for no reason; his hands were sure and deft, and he was proud of it. His astonishing agility kept him in unpaid-for sweets, and he was going to be a pickpocket when he grew up, just like his dad. But unlike his dad, he was not going to get caught.

'Silly ole dip,' he said fondly of his absent father, using the slang term for a pickpocket. His dad had been caught lifting a wallet from a man's pocket and had panicked, pushing him to the ground. What with charges of pickpocketing and assault proven against him, Mr.

O'Brien was beginning a six-month sentence in prison. Joe already missed him something awful.

'Joe,' a high voice called through the trees, 'Mummy says tea's ready.'

He turned at the sound of the baby voice and watched the youngest of the Mallory family trip across the grass. He didn't know her name, and it was a sign of his misery that he had no wish to know. Usually his sharp wits would have had all the Mallorys taped within the first ten minutes of meeting them.

'Did you see Miss Blossom, Joe? She's the most beautiful horse there ever was,' the youngest Mallory piped. 'I hope you didn't go too near because she likes to kick. Daddy says Miss Blossom's bad-tempered and vain. She's been with us as long as I can remember.'

He dropped to the ground, his stomach reacting pleasurably to the idea of Mrs. Mallory's super cooking.

'Horses aren't vain.'

'Miss Blossom is. You have to tell her how pretty she is before she'll do what you want. We love her.'

'How can you love something that tries to kick you?'

'Dunno. We just do.' She took out one of the kittens that she carried in the large pocket of her apron and gave it a damp kiss.

All the Mallorys liked animals, Joe thought as they walked through the orchard. Mr. Mallory was a farmer, growing something or other, and there were chickens, cats, cows, frogs, birds and insects on the farm. Joe was sure that he had been placed in a zoo of nutters, rather than the 'good Christian family' that his social worker had said they were.

There were a great many people on the back lawn when they reached the large farmhouse which sprawled in all directions. They were eating scones and strawberries and drinking tea. Joe brightened. This was afternoon tea, not high tea, and he might get another full meal later. Though he would not have admitted it, he liked Mrs. Mallory's big cooked meals and thought them a great change from the frozen TV suppers he and his dad always ate.

Clive motioned him over. 'Clive of India', he was called. The family had a 'thing' about India. Clive was tall and was various shades of brown from his short cut hair and wide eyes to his tanned skin.

Joe picked out the other three Mallory children from the crowd, the little girl who had fetched him, an older girl and a boy about fifteen. The rest of the kids who were sprawled on the grass seemed to be friends of theirs. Joe began to eat.

Clive said, 'How about biking to the village? Mum needs some shopping.'

Joe shrugged. He couldn't ride a bike, but he wasn't going to tell Clive. Clive probably did everything and did it well; he had that look about him. Clive was twelve years old with quiet eyes and a straight, lithe body that made him look like a born athlete. He wore a smart pair of Rohan bags, grey trousers with loads of open and zippered pockets, and Joe longed for such a pair.

A girl had strolled up, and she dropped on the ground beside them. 'I want to come, too.'

Joe remembered that this particular Mallory was Louisa, named in honour of Louis Mountbatten, one-time Governor of India. Louisa slept next door to Clive and him. Last night she had snored, the only noise that had broken the depressing silence.

'You can't come,' Clive said patiently. 'Joe'll be using the spare bike.' Clive seemed to have unlimited patience. He could prove to be a real pain in the neck. 'Besides, your girl-friends want to play volley-ball.'

And that was another thing! Joe exploded silently. Fancy a house with a garden big enough to play sports! The last time his dad had been in prison, he'd been sent to stay with a family in the city. They'd had a garden, but it had been the size of a postage stamp. They'd been as proud as punch about it and nearly counted the blades of grass every day. The Mallorys used their big garden like it was meant to be a playground. They couldn't be for real!

Louisa raised her rather pudgy figure from the ground. She had round blue eyes in a round face fringed by fair hair. She talked a lot.

'But I need to exercise my leg muscles.' She turned to Joe to say confidentially, 'I'm going to be a fashion model when I grow up.'

Joe nodded but said nothing. This had nothing to do with him. Seeing that no help was at hand, Louisa sighed and ambled away to join her friends.

The Mallorys might not have seemed real, but the bicycle did. Clive's eyebrow rose when Joe slid off the saddle for the third time in as many wobbly minutes, but he said nothing. Joe gritted his teeth and climbed on again. He gave Clive a wild grin. 'I'm going to beat this thing if it takes all night.'

The older boy looked as if he wanted to laugh but he didn't, and some minutes later when Joe had come to terms with balance, he said, 'You're doing fine, not many kids learn to ride as fast as you are.'

Presently Joe felt confident enough to spare a look around him as they pedalled along. It was a waste of time. There was nothing to see but trees and grass, and more grass. He groaned inwardly at the dullness of it all. They passed a weather-beaten sign at the entrance to a dirt track which curved away into the hills. It read 'Oak Acres'. A sign of life!

Clive noticed his interest. 'Deserted farm,' he said. 'The last owner moved out after he ran it into the ground.'

Joe thought it over. 'I reckon he was carted away in a strait-jacket, a screaming loony from all the quiet.'

Clive laughed until he had to pull up at the side of

the road. 'You don't say much, Joe, but when you do, it's worth hearing!'

The village nearest to Windrush Farm was a collection of grey stone houses edging a tarmac road with a sprinkling of shops to serve the surrounding agricultural area. They propped the bikes against a wall. Not so much as a chain to secure them, Joe thought, as they walked away. At home they'd probably be nicked by the time he and Clive got back. He shook his head wonderingly.

The general store was called The Village Pantry and sold a bit of everything, including sweets. Clive checked his list and found a basket. Joe wandered off on his own. It was time to stock up on chocolate.

He flexed his fingers while he looked casually around. A man was serving a woman at the counter and talking to her. A second woman was bent over the food freezer and another one was leaving the shop. No one was paying any attention to him, and he went over to the display of sweets.

His heart began to thud unpleasantly. His mouth was dry as ashes, but his hands were damp. He rubbed his right palm against his jeans to dry it. His hand snaked out and as quick as lightning a bar of chocolate disappeared into the generous pocket of his jacket. He looked around again, turning vaguely but in reality checking all directions. No one had noticed a thing. He had not lost any of the old touch, he thought in satisfaction. Now one more for good luck. Another limbering up of his fingers and a second bar joined the first.

Suddenly he sensed that someone was watching him, and he looked up. Clive had come up in his cat-quiet way and stood there, his eyes big and startled. Casually Joe took out the second bar and put his hand back in his pocket to bring out some coins.

He gave Clive his best grin. 'Nearly forgot this costs money.' Hadn't Dad always said to brazen it out if you got caught? He held his breath and waited for what Clive would do.

Clive looked a little confused and frowned, but he started toward the cash desk without a word. Joe couldn't believe his luck. Clive was going to give him the benefit of a doubt even though he *must* have seen him filch the chocolate! Joe remembered something else that Dad had said, something about people not being willing to believe what they saw. Clive might *look* like he was a champ, but he had a lot to learn. Joe could have hugged himself as he paid his bill.

Outside the bikes were still propped against the wall. Clive packed the shopping into his saddle bag, they mounted and started back to Windrush Farm. Joe decided to play it cool. He puckered up his lips to whistle, but nothing came out. Why couldn't he whistle like he had done on the way there? Not only had he got away with it back in the shop but he had another bar of chocolate in his pocket that Clive knew nothing about. He'd won, but for the life of him he couldn't raise a sound.

Clive had joked a lot on the way to the village, but now he looked straight ahead at the road. At length he said slowly, 'A man and his wife bought that shop last year, and Dad says they're running it on a shoestring. Every penny counts. Mum tries to shop there as much as she can. They're nice people, and well liked.'

Clive rode on a while before he added, 'The man's a Falklands war veteran. He was shot up pretty bad and spent a long time in hospital before he got invalided out of the Marines.'

Joe felt his face burn.

The big kitchen table was loaded with good things to eat at supper-time. Joe's mouth began to water at the sight of the platters of roast chicken, salad and cheese.

There were maybe a dozen people around the big table, young and old. Louisa looked as hungry as Joe felt, and the younger girl was talking down to the kittens in her pocket. Clive studied his empty plate and refused to meet Joe's eye.

At the head of the table Mr. Mallory, a big man with his face burned brown by the sun, folded his hands and bent his head. 'Dear Heavenly Father,' he began.

Joe groaned inwardly. He was starving and they had to wait while Mr. Mallory prayed! This family didn't seem to do anything without first checking with God.

Mr. Mallory went on. 'We thank you for this food and for each other and for the happiness that is ours. We thank you for sending us Joseph O'Brien to share our lives and pray that he will find the joy of living that is ours. Amen.'

Everyone said 'Amen' and the food started round the table.

'Joy of living!' thought Joe scornfully. 'I'm happy like I am. I don't need to find out anything from this bunch!'

2

Joe turned over in bed and punched his pillow. He turned back and tried to wriggle his toes, one at a time. He couldn't, but it passed the time. He eventually returned to staring at the lighter square that was the window. The small bedroom under the eaves of the farmhouse was otherwise dark, and the heat of the day was still heavy.

In the other bed Clive was asleep and had been since five minutes after lights out. The rest of the Mallorys had trailed off to bed at various times. Joe knew that for a fact, because he had counted them coming up the stairs, one by one.

Something black and big flew by the window. Joe almost wished it were a bat; he'd invite it in and wrestle a round with Count Dracula. Anything to break the dreary silence that was as total as anything he could remember. Silence, that is, if you could forget Louisa's snores from the bedroom next door.

What he wouldn't give for the familiar rumble of traffic, the overhead whine of a jet engine, the screech of a police car!

Joe's ears pricked up. Underlying the adenoidal snores from Louisa was another sound. He tossed aside the covers, hurried to the open window and leaned out. No mistake, the low sound of a well-tuned car engine came through the black night. Joe waited to be diverted from his boredom.

The volume of sound increased slightly and Joe frowned, searching for the source. The car lights ought to be clear by now, but they were not. His gaze flicked back and forth along the narrow lane. There – something was moving, a bulky, spooky shape.

The sound came close and his eyes widened in astonishment. It was a car all right, but without any lights showing. Furthermore, it seemed that all the chrome trim had been blacked out because not so much as a glint showed. Dangerous, he thought.

The car passed the house. Not a car, he realised from its vague outline, but a Land Rover. And it was pulling a horse box, also without a light of any kind showing. Peculiar. Stupid but curious. Joe shook his head and trailed back to bed.

He considered what kind of a spooky place this was where people drove their cars in the dead of night, pulling horse boxes, so quietly and furtively that only city lads who couldn't sleep would see them. No real answer had come to mind when suddenly he was asleep.

Joe felt bleary and sandy-eyed when Louisa shook him awake with a cup of tea. 'It's morning,' she said unnecessarily. 'Time to get up.'

He gasped and pulled the covers over his head.

'Don't be daft,' she said, putting the tea on the floor beside him. 'I've seen boys in pyjamas before.'

'Not me!' came the muffled reply.

When he peered over the covers a short time later she had gone, and Clive was there instead, fully dressed and making his bed. 'I'll be out in the yard, Joe, starting the chores. The quicker we start, the quicker we finish,' he called as he left.

Clive sounded as offhand as he had last night, Joe decided. Come to think of it Clive had been offhand ever since they left The Village Pantry yesterday. Maybe Clive was sharper than he thought. Maybe the 'forgot to pay' line hadn't completely laid Clive's suspicion to rest.

Joe shrugged. No matter. Clive would get over it.

He got up, washed and dressed. He smoothed the bedcovers in the same way that his room-mate had done but without the same tidy results. The O'Briens didn't go in much for making beds. He drank the tea while he watered his tray of geranium cuttings.

Louisa sped by the open door, did a double-take and skidded back. 'What're you doing?'

'Looking after my dad's geraniums. He's good at flowers and stuff.' He pinched off a dead leaf and poked at the earth. He had wanted to bring all Dad's plants from the flat, but his social worker had allowed only these. The others had been distributed to the neighbours. His dad wouldn't like that, but Joe had done his best.

'They look healthy,' she remarked. Joe showed her the plant food his dad used. 'That's good stuff but expensive. We'll fix you up with something else. Finished?'

'Yeah.'

'Then let's go.'

There were chickens to feed and eggs to collect, a cow to bring from pasture and milk, and pets to feed. The fifteen-year-old Mallory boy was off with his father doing something important to a field.

Louisa handed him the basket of eggs they had collected. 'Mum needs these. You can take them in.' He did so, sniffing appreciatively at the warm smells of breakfast when he entered the house. His stomach liked Mrs. Mallory's preparations for breakfast.

When Joe came out Louisa was whispering to Clive and shaking a forefinger, and he was scowling. They both stopped when Joe hove into view.

'Come on, Joe,' Clive said coolly. 'You can give me a hand with the tractor.'

Louisa nodded in approval. 'I'll bet Joe knows all about engines.'

'Nope,' said Joe mildly.

Clive sighed. 'You can hand me the tools. The carburettor needs adjusting.'

Clive made the delicate adjustments to the engine part

while Joe handed him the tools. Watching the deft way Clive handled the tools, it occurred to him that Clive had all the makings of a first class pickpocket. And not only was he good with his hands but he had a careful, controlled way of walking. He could be in and out of a crowd with half a dozen wallets and purses and never be noticed. Joe was struck with admiration.

Clive gave a final listen to the raucous engine, decided it was satisfactory and switched off. 'That should do, but Dad'll double check later.'

They returned to the house to wash. Joe said, 'Funny thing happened last night after you were asleep. A Land Rover with a horse box went by.'

'So?'

Joe coloured at his indifference. 'I know they're a penny a dozen around here, but this one wasn't showing a light.'

'Hmm,' said Clive, turning on the taps of the wash basin and handing Joe the soap.

'Seems peculiar,' Joe persisted.

'Could be. Hurry up, Mum's calling breakfast.'

So that was that, Joe thought. Clive was not interested in the news about the nocturnal traveller and all because he was worried about one crummy bar of chocolate. It was weird how some people went on about things!

Mr. Mallory and the elder boy, who had the big square look of his dad, sat down at the kitchen table. The boy was called Kip, after Rudyard Kipling, the famous author who wrote about India. Joe had figured out that connection with India by himself.

Mr. Mallory thanked God for the meal. This time Joe didn't mind. After an hour spent close to the farm animals, he felt kind of different – close to nature, so to speak. Maybe God and nature went hand in hand, he decided, feeling generous. Country people were bound to feel differently from city people about God.

The dishes of food were passed around and Joe tucked

into a plate heaped with every good thing he could imagine that a breakfast should have.

Louisa elbowed him. 'I'm not going to be a fashion model. I changed my mind,' she said confidentially.

'Overnight?' he muttered in surprise.

'Overnight, overday, who cares? The thing is I realized I love hot buttered toast, and nobody in her right mind who loves hot buttered toast should even think about being a fashion model.'

It made sense. 'Hmm,' said Joe, borrowing Clive's remark.

'Instead I'm going to take speech lessons and be a television newsreader. I already have five pounds put away. I'd saved it for a modelling course, but it'll do for speech lessons instead. Pass the marmalade.'

'You always change your mind about things?'

'Only about my future. It's important, you know.' Her round face was serious and her blue eyes intent.

'I guess.' And that was not strictly true because he had thought a lot about his own future. He knew what he was going to be. A pickpocket just like his dad. He hugged the knowledge to himself with pride.

After breakfast Louisa took him upstairs to her bedroom and rummaged in her wardrobe. 'I've got lots of stuff I never play with any more.'

Joe bridled. What did he want with dolls?

But he had underestimated Louisa's common sense. She unearthed a magic set. 'Last year I was going to be a lady magician, but I kind of lost interest.' She thrust the box into his hands. 'It's yours, Joe. If you want it.'

He grinned, more from the pleasure of receiving than with any real enthusiasm for what it was. 'Let's have a look.'

He spread the contents on the table. There were cups, little soft balls, playing cards and thick string – *everything for the junior magician*, the instruction book read. It was great!

Joe beamed. 'Give you a quid for it.'

She was faintly shocked. 'But it's a present!'

Clive's voice came from the doorway. 'Louisa's giving it to you, Joe.' He came in and flicked through the items on the table. ''Course you don't have to take it. It's not all that fantastic.'

Joe's lips tightened. 'It's terrific, and I do want it. Thanks, Louisa.'

Unaccountably Clive grinned. 'That's okay then. Think you can do any of the tricks?'

Joe flipped through the booklet. Tricks that took a secret partner in the audience did not interest him, but the sleight of hand stuff looked interesting. It depended on some clever hand work, and he knew all about clever hand work.

He decided to try the Astonishing String Trick. The idea was to cut a piece of string in two and at the finish produce the string again, magically back in one piece. He read through the instructions and chuckled. Cheeky, really cheeky!

He looked up to see the youngest Mallory, kitten in hand, regarding him solemnly from behind her brother. Her name was Vicky, he had learned, named after Victoria, Empress of India. Naturally. Vicky was little and kind of pink.

So he had a proper audience. Joe straightened to his full height.

'Ladies and gentleman,' he intoned, caught up in the fun of the moment. The others blinked and exchanged smiles.

'Be seated.' Joe waved to the bed. 'You are about to witness the miracle of the century. Before your very eyes you will see a wonder of the world of magic that will mystify and delight.' The words poured out from some theatrical part of his mind, and his audience loved it. Louisa squealed, Vicky hugged her kitten and Clive laughed.

'I shall take this piece of string – ' He held it up, measuring it between his hands, 'cut it in two with a sharp pair of fine scissors. And then, and then I shall with a mysterious process known only to the fakirs of deepest India, restore the cut string to its original form.'

He folded the string in half with elaborate care and placed it against his open palm and closed his hand. The loop showed above his fist. The two ends dangled below. His audience watched, wide-eyed.

He turned to the table and picked up the scissors. 'And with these, I cut the loop.' He showed them the scissors. 'Like this.' With a snip the curved continuous loop above his fist became two separate pieces of string.

'Oh!' gasped Vicky.

'But now, I say the magic words, "abracadabra, heavy metal pop, iced lollies and caramels" and – ' He pulled the string from his hand.

Vicky shrieked in delight. The string was whole again. Everybody clapped like mad, and Joe bowed.

'How did you do it?' they demanded.

Joe shrugged modestly. 'Easy. There were two pieces of string in my hand. One string made the loop, the other one showed below my fist as the two ends. I cut the top one that had the loop, but afterwards I showed you the bottom one, the string that was always whole.'

'Easy enough, so you say,' Louisa followed on promptly, 'but the fact is you were terrific, and I never saw you palm the second piece of string. Did you, Clive?'

'Never. Great stuff.'

'I palmed it when I picked up the scissors,' Joe said.

'More,' cried Vicky.

Joe said, 'Later, when I've studied up and practised a little.'

The party broke up, and Joe took the magic set into the orchard next to Miss Blossom's paddock. He read aloud to the grazing horse and practised rolling the ping pong ball through his fingers.

Miss Blossom ignored him. Joe didn't mind. The sound of her munching and the soft thud of her heavy hooves on the grass was the perfect background to his work.

After a big midday dinner Mrs. Mallory sent Clive into the village for baking powder. Joe strolled after him to the barn where the bicycles were kept. He would never ask to go along, but he would make himself available.

Clive saw him and a shadow passed across his face. 'D'you want to come?' he asked and gave him a searching look.

Joe could not meet his eyes. 'I guess.' He mounted the other bicycle and led the way down the lane.

Nothing had changed along the way. There was still the same old dreary view of trees and bushes and grass. Birds twittered and insects darted. The hot sun made the tarmac a bit sticky.

They passed the deserted Oak Acres and Clive said, 'I wonder when the farm's going up for sale. Old man Winkle moved out last month, but there's no For Sale sign yet. You'd think he'd want to put it on the market quick, broke as he was.'

'Seems likely.' But Joe was not interested.

They rounded the final curve before the village and Joe's gaze fastened on a Land Rover entering the main street. There was something disturbingly familiar about it. 'Clive, look at that Rover.'

It was just disappearing around a corner.

'Where?'

'You missed it, but I think it's the same one I saw last night. You remember, the one with no lights. That one,' he let go the handlebar to point toward the corner, 'was dark and dirty, all the chrome bits covered with mud.'

They parked their bikes near The Village Pantry. Clive's face was tight and his eyes worried. He kept glancing at the shop and down at the ground. 'Lots of

Rovers need a wash. Besides you were probably dreaming last night,' he said dismissively.

Joe stiffened. 'I wasn't dreaming.'

'So you say. You coming in?' Clive asked in a tense voice.

Joe set his mouth. He was quietly furious. Clive hadn't believed a word he'd said. 'I'll wait here.'

Clive's expression lightened. 'Right. Won't be a minute.'

None of Joe's anger had abated by the time they returned to Windrush Farm. Clive had just the same as called him a liar.

He put away the bicycle and without a word strode off to pour out his resentment to Miss Blossom, the only one in a hundred miles who would listen to the injustice of it all.

He sat on the fence and complained, 'Just because I take sweets, does that make me a liar?'

Miss Blossom turned her head and sneered.

'I know what I saw and I saw that very Land Rover roll by here after midnight without a single light showing.'

He absently held out an apple from the orchard. Miss Blossom took it, trying to nip his hand at the same time.

'Ungrateful old cow!' he called, startled.

Her head lifted and she fixed him with a haughty stare, coming ominously close to his perch on the fence. He scrambled down. 'No offence, Miss Blossom. Sorry. You're still the most beautiful thing I've ever seen.' She gave him a long look and began to graze again.

'You're something, all right,' he laughed.

From among the trees Louisa called to him. 'We're going swimming. Meet you at the river.'

Joe's brown eyes lit up and he set off for the house to change.

When he reached the river Clive and Louisa were already in the water and some distance away. It was an idle kind of river, not wide, quiet and dreamy and slow moving. Vicky sat on the bank, playing with her kittens. She smiled when Joe hurried up.

'These babies run away and chase butterflies instead of learning to jump. Naughty babies,' she scolded fondly.

Joe jumped into the water. Despite the sun's heat, the water was cold. Maybe a hundred degrees colder than the swimming baths at home, he groaned. He swam furiously to warm himself. When he next glanced toward the bank, Vicky was at the edge of the water with a determined look on her pink face, chasing a kitten.

'Vicky, watch it!' he called, instinctively sensing danger.

She lunged for the scampering animal, lost her balance and without a word fell sideways into the water.

Joe shouted and started toward her, cutting swiftly through the water. His heart was in his mouth. Vicky was going to drown, and the others were too far away to do anything about it. Saving the kid was up to him, and he would never reach her in time because his skinny arms wouldn't move fast enough! A part of him knew that he was moving as fast as any fish, but it didn't seem so. He seemed to be swimming in slow motion.

She sank out of sight.

He dug deep inside himself, found a burst of speed, reached the spot where she had disappeared and stood up.

The water was not deep there, but it was too deep for Vicky, he thought desperately. There was no sign of her. Where had she drifted? Think! his mind screamed through the horror, and the answer came: she had drifted in the direction of the lazy current.

He launched himself downstream and found Vicky at once, clinging to some long weeds.

He took one little fat arm in a firm grasp and brought her up to the surface beside him. Her eyes were squeezed shut and her lips pressed tight. The water rolled off her hair and face.

By the time he pushed her up onto the bank, Louisa and Clive were beside them, white-faced with fright.

Louisa cried, 'Vicky, are you all right?' Clive looked like he might be sick any second.

Joe said softly, 'Vicky, you can open your eyes now.'

The cornflower blue eyes popped open immediately, her face crumpled, and she let out a bellowing howl that rolled around the trees and sent the birds winging skyward. No music had sounded so sweet to his ears.

Louisa's shoulders slumped in relief. 'She's okay.'

Clive's hand came down on his shoulder. 'Thanks.'

Joe coloured hotly. He was not used to gratitude. 'That's okay,' he mumbled.

Louisa took charge. 'That's enough for today. Everybody back to the house.'

3

By the time Vicky had been wrapped in a towel and the kittens caught, some time passed, enough time for Joe to find his composure. He had been terrified. He could admit that to himself because he had seen Clive's bloodless face which must have been the colour of his own.

At the house Vicky was handed over to her mother. Joe bore Mrs. Mallory's hugs and thanks with fortitude, but he slipped away when she began a stern lecture to Clive and Louisa on the folly of leaving their young sister alone. He felt sick now that it was over, and after he changed into his clothes he lay down on his bed.

Presently Clive arrived with hot, sweet tea. They drank in silence. Joe felt better.

At last Clive said, 'Let's go and see Miss Blossom.'

Joe could hardly believe his ears. Clive sounded really friendly! Gone was the reserve he had shown since The Village Pantry incident. He was smiling, and his eyes were warm.

Clive went on, suddenly red-faced. 'I guess I owe you an apology. I thought the other afternoon that maybe you were trying to steal that chocolate. I was wrong. I'm sorry.'

'That's okay,' he mumbled.

He could have laughed aloud. Clive had not trusted his own eyes after all! Clive really and truly thought that anyone who pulled Vicky out of the river could not steal! Clive was wrong, of course, but he was not going to tell him.

Joe jumped to his feet. 'Let's go. I want to see you ride the vainest horse in the world.'

They went off to the paddock well pleased with each other.

That night as Joe showered he thought about the wonderful afternoon with Clive. That boy could ride! He had whistled and Miss Blossom had trotted to him, meek as a lamb. Clive had jumped up on her back easy as pie and ridden her bareback all around the paddock. Miss Blossom had even seemed pleased at his attention.

Joe had fed her apples, and not once had she tried to bite him. Then for his own part in the fun, Joe had demonstrated the new trick he was practising and plucked a coin from behind Clive's ear. Joe had shown him how it was done, hiding the coin between his fingers and producing it at the right time. Clive had enjoyed it.

When he returned to the bedroom, Clive was on his knees beside his bed, saying his prayers.

Joe watched him for a long moment, then climbed into bed. If his friend – he liked the word and repeated it to himself – if his new friend wanted to finish each day in that odd way, well, that was all right. Praying was not for the likes of Joe O'Brien, but his friend could do what he liked.

The light went out, Clive fell asleep and Joe listened to Louisa's snores from the next room.

He must have been dozing when he heard the low, well-tuned engine of a car. His eyes shot open and he scrambled to the window. This was the same sound he had heard before. Clive had not believed him then, but now he would be made to believe.

Joe sped to the other bed and shook him awake. 'It's coming, the same car as before.'

Clive snorted awake. 'What's up?'

'The same car, coming now, be quick – '

Clive groaned, crawled out of bed and staggered across the room.

'Listen,' Joe cautioned.

Clive rubbed his eyes and leaned out of the window. The sound was near. 'Any second now,' whispered Joe.

The strange caravan passed again in the night, the Land Rover without lights travelling slowly, quietly, and pulling a horse box, equally dark. They watched until a bend in the road hid it from sight.

'How about that!' Clive breathed.

'So what d'you think?' Joe asked when they had gone back to their beds.

'Haven't a clue. What about you?'

'Snap.'

'Has to be a reason. Maybe his electrics broke down.'

'Maybe.' Joe sounded as doubtful as Clive had. A complete failure of lights demanded instant repairs.

'Or maybe it's something from outer space.'

'D'you mind!' said Joe with heavy scorn.

Clive chuckled. 'Go to sleep.'

And strangely enough Joe did.

The two boys discussed it again the next morning while doing their chores, but no satisfactory explanation resulted. They forgot about the mysterious midnight traveller in the following days.

Joe swam, helped around the farm, ate Mrs. Mallory's good cooking and often visited Miss Blossom. She remained aloof and bad tempered, but he didn't mind. It was enough to watch her lovely mane flow when she galloped and the toss of her proud head when she noticed him.

All the Mallorys went to church each Sunday in the village. Mr. Mallory made it clear that Joe was not obliged to go with them, but when two lonely Sunday mornings had passed on his own, he tagged along. Mr. and Mrs. Mallory were pleased, and Joe was glad that he had offered.

He found that he liked the service. He didn't know what was happening or why, but he liked the feel of the old village church and the music. He spent most of his time looking at the pictures in the stained glass windows.

What with the organ music surging into the high vaulted ceiling and the sun pouring through the coloured glass, Joe thought of his father with a pain of regret. How he wished that Dad were with him to share this.

When they returned to the farmhouse, Joe asked for a postcard and wrote to his father. He printed the card carefully because he had long ago caught on that Mr. O'Brien didn't read or write well. His dad didn't know his numbers either, and Joe had quietly taken on the job of budgeting their unsteady income.

He wrote about the geranium cuttings and added a PS. 'I wish you could work in the garden because time might pass quicker, doing something you like.'

He left the card on the hall table for posting, collected his cigarettes and went out in the garden for a smoke.

Under a tree out of view of the house he lit up. The first puff tasted foul, but he carried on because in his neighbourhood smoking meant that you were cool, street-wise, knowing. The second puff started him coughing. He watched the tobacco disappear in ash and wondered how much of Dad's hard-earned cash was going up in smoke.

Clive sat down beside him. 'Hi.' He, too, watched Mr. O'Brien's hard-earned, if illegal, cash disappear in smoke and ash.

Joe coughed again. 'Want one?'

'No thanks. You don't seem to want one either.'

'I'll get used to it.'

'Why?'

'It's what kids do if they want to look cool.'

Clive considered it. 'But why do *you* smoke? You're cool as they come.'

It was a simple question, but Joe's head swivelled around to meet his friend's enquiring look. 'Am I?' he asked, pleased as punch. He decided that he'd suffered enough for one day and stubbed out the cigarette. 'But you're cooler.'

Clive punched his shoulder. 'In a pig's eye.'

It seemed a good idea to wrestle over the difference of opinion, and for the next few minutes they butted each other and slipped in and out of holds in high good humour. Clive was bigger but Joe held his own and both gave a good account of themselves.

When they finished and sprawled panting on the grass, Clive said, 'Sometimes I think you know a lot more than I do. And I don't mean stuff like maths.'

'That's 'cause I live where I do,' Joe replied shrewdly. 'You have to be sharp or you'd never go out.'

'Sounds rough.'

'I like it,' Joe said.

Joe's lips twisted. He tossed the box of cigarettes to his friend. 'Okay, no more smokes. You win.'

Clive caught it, screwed up the box and stuffed it in a pocket. 'Wrong. You're the winner because you did the right thing.'

The annual church picnic took place two Saturdays later, and Joe awoke that morning with the expectation of a super time ahead. He and Clive had spent the previous day on the green next to the village church, helping to string bunting, set up the barbecue and prepare the children's games.

The occasion would be small potatoes compared to the big events held in the city, but Joe had liked the low-key bustle on the green. He had known many of the people helping through attending the Sunday services with the Mallorys, and feeling a part of things was good. The last firework display he had been to with Dad, he had been one of fifty thousand strangers. Dad, incidentally, had made a packet that night, sliding through the distracted crowd and lifting wallets as he went.

He was already dressed when Clive awoke. 'Sun's shining,' he grinned.

'Great.'

They fed the animals and finished their chores in double-quick time.

Mid-morning they drove to the green, parked the car and unloaded the food. The aroma of meat sizzling on the barbecue grills slipped along Joe's nostrils and kicked his taste buds into high gear. Groups of people stood about talking, children chased each other until they were red in the face and collapsed in shrieking heaps.

Joe and Clive wandered, hands in pockets, feeling vastly superior. 'Bunting looks good,' Clive said with a judicious look.

'Some idiot's already torn it down from that tree,' added Joe.

They strolled around a group of men, close in conversation, and Joe whisked himself up into the tree to re-tie the broken string.

Mr. Mallory was in the group of local farmers. He rubbed his square jaw consideringly and said, 'It's been going on for some weeks now.'

'Bad business,' remarked another.

Joe and Clive exchanged puzzled looks. What was 'bad business'?

'They're shipped off to the continent. Or so the papers reckon,' remarked the third man. 'Big market for horse meat across the Channel.'

'A delicacy I'm told,' added Mr. Mallory.

Joe's stomach heaved and he nearly fell from the tree. Horse meat a delicacy? People *ate* horses!

He stared down into Clive's equally appalled eyes.

The second man in the group spoke up again. 'No reason not to, I suppose, horses are plant eaters just like cattle, but all the same, it wouldn't do for me.'

A picture of Miss Blossom flashed through Joe's mind. Nor for me, his mind screamed silently.

'Well, this is something new. Horse rustling. I've heard of sheep rustling in Wales and some cattle stealing up in Scotland, but horse rustling? And in the very next county? Beats all!'

The men moved away, and Joe climbed down from the tree. He swallowed hard.

Clive brushed the sweat off his forehead with the back of his hand. 'I feel sick.'

'I feel – I feel – ' Joe broke off, his hands working convulsively.

'I know. I feel the same. When I think of Miss Blossom – '

'Don't!' protested Joe. 'If I thought of Miss Blossom on a butcher's block, I'd bust wide open.'

The boys walked slowly back to the tables, gazing down at their shoes.

It was lucky that they were hungry and were faced with countless tempting dishes. The shocking conversation they had overheard passed into the back of their minds when choosing between the Sunday School teacher's honey baked ham and hamburgers fresh off the grill. They played safe and had some of each.

By mid-afternoon the remains of the meal had been cleared away and the games were under way.

Clive was running in the cross-country race. He admitted that it was not so much 'cross-country' as around a hill and back again, but it sounded good. The course was such that it had to be marked out with little red flags on poles. Joe and Louisa were in charge of such a course marker at a V-junction.

'Wouldn't do to go the wrong way,' commented Louisa.

'Clive could double-back and still win,' Joe said bracingly.

Clive grinned. Joe thought he looked a little nervous.

There were a dozen boys in the long race, milling around the starting line. Time was called. Joe shouldered the binoculars which he had remembered to borrow from Kip, and he and Louisa hurried to their position.

It was a good spot. Far enough from the starting line to watch the straight first run, but close enough to the marker to rush there when the racers neared the curve.

Joe uncased the binoculars and walked back to the bend to focus on the starting line.

He was interested in the lad next to Clive. Taller than Clive, longer legs, probably a good runner. His name was Al Bailey, a new-comer who would be in Clive's year when school started. His brother was a champion cricketer. Al frowned, his eyes were never still, and Joe didn't trust him an inch.

On the starting line there was a lot of jostling for position. Joe caught his breath. Just as he thought. Al was giving Clive a hard time. And Clive was taking it with a grin, like he didn't know the difference between jostling and shoving.

Louisa came up. 'Have they started?'

'Not yet,' Joe said in a strange voice.

'Anything the matter?' she asked in alarm.

'There – they're off. Go back to the marker, I'll be along.'

He gripped the binoculars and watched closely. Clive and Al quickly broke clear of the others and ran side by side in easy strides, not too fast because the race was a long one. Al could run, all right, but so could Clive. It would be a toss-up who would win.

Clive and Al were some distance from the starting line. Joe had started to lower the binoculars but he caught his breath and jammed them against his eyes again. Al had deliberately swerved into Clive. Clive stumbled and lurched sideways off the course. Al shot ahead.

'You ratfink!' Joe muttered. He ran to join Louisa. 'They're coming.'

'About time. I'm half asleep standing here. Joe, what're you doing!' she gasped.

Joe was pulling up the flag marker. 'Help me,' he ordered grimly.

'Are you nuts?'

Louisa was a chatterbox, but she was no fool. She saw Joe's black look and without a word helped move the flag to the other track. 'The runners will follow the wrong course,' she reminded him.

'Only one of them. Just hold the pole still and look important.'

'But this is cheating!'

Al came tearing around the bend of the hill, saw the flag and the two figures standing stiffly beside it, and promptly headed along the wrong path.

'Move it back again,' whispered Joe.

'What's going on?' she moaned as they hurried to their proper position.

Joe didn't answer. More runners appeared, among them Clive, trailing badly and running awkwardly. He seemed to have hurt his leg.

'Go get 'em,' Louisa cheered her brother.

But clearly, because of Al's treachery, he no longer had a chance.

When the last of the twelve runners passed, Joe and Louisa carried the marker flag to the finish line to watch the results.

'So what was that all about?' Louisa demanded along the way.

'Al pushed Clive off the track. I saw it through the binoculars. I tried to even up the odds.'

Louisa looked at him in shock. 'You can't be serious!'

'Knock it off,' he said bitterly, remembering that once Clive had also doubted his word. 'I saw what I saw, and Al deliberately pushed Clive.'

Her round eyes tightened with anger.

Clive was fourth to finish.

'Bad luck,' Joe said.

'It happens,' Clive gasped out as he panted.

Joe looked at him in surprise. Could it be that he didn't realise what had happened?

Al steamed in. He looked surprised to see that he was the last to finish. Everyone else did, too, and he stamped away in a temper.

'Wonder what happened to Al?' Clive remarked.

Louisa turned pink and Joe looked away.

4

Clive and Joe were finishing lemonades when Al rolled up, scarlet with anger. He stepped up to Joe and stuck out his chin. 'What d'you mean, sending me off the wrong way? Thought I wouldn't figure it out, did you? Well, I did, and you're a cheat!' He planted a hand on Joe's thin chest and pushed hard. The smaller boy went staggering back.

Clive stepped between them. 'That's enough, Al. Pick on somebody your own size.'

Joe hurled back into the fray. 'Stay clear, it's between Al and me.'

'That'll be the day. Okay, Al, what's the problem?'

Al jabbed his finger at Joe. 'Him! He moved the marker at the junction so I'd go off in the wrong direction. I'd have won if it hadn't been for him!'

Clive turned to his friend. 'What d'you say to that?'

Joe shrugged. 'True I changed the marker. Whether he would've won is something else.' Clive's tanned face darkened a few shades.

Joe ignored him. He tapped the binoculars and looked straight at Al. 'I saw what happened. You deliberately pushed Clive, and he went down.'

Al stopped blustering. 'It was an accident.'

'Accident, my foot! You went out of your way to get near him and then shoved him. You got what you deserved, Al, so call it quits.' Joe felt hot and righteous, and when Al shot him a final angry look and sloped off, he thought to himself 'Good riddance'.

'You were wrong,' Clive said flatly. 'There was no cause to cheat.'

Joe bristled. 'If you'd kept your eyes open, there wouldn't have been any reason to even the odds.'

Clive put his fists on his hips. 'Just what d'you mean by that?'

'You should've known Al was out to get you. The way he shoved you around at the starting line – '

'Everybody was jostling everybody,' Clive interrupted.

'That bully was shoving you right, left and centre! Not everybody is as straightforward as you Mallorys, and you ought to wake up to it!'

Clive retorted, 'All right, so maybe he was shoving, but Christians don't change markers.'

Joe met the blazing eyes and his stinging retort died on his lips. Maybe Clive was right. Maybe he should have done nothing, just stood by and let Al win hands down by cheating. Clive was a Christian, and Clive should know.

No, Clive was wrong, Joe thought suddenly. Mr. Mallory was a Christian, too, the finest man he knew next to his dad, and Mr. Mallory stood up for what he knew was right. He wasn't loud, but he was firm. Everybody liked and respected him, and he would never let anybody get away with something bad if he could help it.

Joe calmed down. 'Christians have to live in the real world, too, and going around with your head in the sand isn't the answer,' he said evenly.

Clive bit his lip and colour flooded his face. 'All right, so Al pushed me off the track. That doesn't mean I can't take care of myself. I don't need some skinny kid to step in.'

Clive was embarrassed and fast working himself into a rage. 'One thing I learned today for sure. You *were* stealing the chocolate from The Village Pantry! I thought it wasn't possible, but it's true! You're a sneak thief, and I don't want your help. Ever!'

Joe stood frozen to the spot as Clive whirled around

and strode swiftly away. Deep inside he felt a knife-twist of hurt so painful that his hands went to his stomach. He walked into the deep shadow of the nearby trees.

When he was out of sight of the picnic, he sank to the earth. His lips tightened and he brushed fiercely at his eyes. He would not cry. He never cried, and he would not start now. Clive had no right to say those things. He'd only tried to help.

Sneak thief! Clive had said.

Joe's fingers curled into fists, and a wave of white hot rage washed over him.

The picnic finished and Joe and the Mallorys returned home.

He didn't speak to Clive the rest of the day, nor did Clive speak to him, but with the bustle of clearing away the picnic, checking the animals, and saying goodbye to Kip who was off to stay with friends, no one seemed to notice anything amiss.

The next day Mrs. Mallory sent the boys on an errand into the nearby town. If she saw the coolness between her son and her charge, she didn't comment but talked cheerfully of the jobs they were to do.

In total silence Clive and Joe caught the bus at the crossroads and rode into town. Without exchanging a word they returned library books, filled the shopping list and went into Woolies for sewing cotton. There Joe went his own way.

A few minutes later Clive found him at the sweet counter. 'Turn out your pockets,' he demanded quietly, but his eyes blazed.

Joe turned out his pockets. Clive took the five packets of sweets that Joe had intended to steal and marched to the pay desk. Joe followed, sullen and scowling.

Clive added the sweets to his own purchases and paid for the lot.

At home Clive frog-marched the struggling, defiant Joe into the orchard. 'Right,' he shouted. 'Why'd you do it this time?'

'Dunno.'

'Don't give me that. You're sharp. You know the "why" for everything you do and say.' He shook him impatiently.

Joe bridled and pulled away. 'None of your business why I was browned off.'

'So every time you feel browned off, you steal! The rest of us heave rocks at the river but you steal!' He pushed at Joe, and Joe went sprawling.

Joe picked himself up, ran full tilt at Clive and butted him in the stomach. Clive went down with a whoosh and bounded up again.

'And I pray for you every night, Joe O'Brien.' He swung his right fist.

Joe ducked and returned his own right, grazing Clive's ear. 'I don't need your prayers. I'm happy like I am.'

Clive took Joe's nose between thumb and forefinger. 'I saw you stealing, remember? You looked like a death's head. You were *not* happy.' He twisted hard and Joe kicked him.

Clive let go and Joe planted a facer. The two boys rolled on the grass, thumping and pummelling until they were too exhausted to go on.

Joe lay on his back, panting, and stared up at the sky. Not like the other time they had wrestled on the grass, he thought. He felt as miserable as he had on the day Dad was sentenced to six months.

He said finally, 'You've got blood on your face.'

Clive rolled over and came to his feet. 'So d'you.' They went to the river and washed before returning to the house.

Going into dinner Mr. Mallory took one look at the two boys and asked quietly, 'Fighting?'

Both shook their heads vigorously. 'Just fooling around,' said Clive.

Joe added, 'We slipped.'

'Quite,' said Mr. Mallory, wisely accepting the explanation. 'No need to fight to settle a difference. God gave us brains to sort things out without hurting each other with our fists.' They went to the big table in the kitchen, Mr. Mallory gave thanks and the meal began.

Louisa was too full of her own problem to appreciate the boys' grazes and withdrawn looks. 'I've looked and looked, and I can't find my money,' she complained. 'I put it in my top drawer, I'm sure I did.'

Everybody knew she meant her savings for speech lessons. Mr. Mallory said, 'Look again, poppet. You're always changing places and forgetting where you last put your money.'

Joe glanced at Clive and froze. Clive was white-faced and stared accusingly at him before looking down at his plate.

Joe's heart fell. Clive believed that he had stolen Louisa's savings! But he hadn't touched her five pounds, had never seen it!

After the meal finished and the table was cleared he slipped away to visit Miss Blossom. The mare would listen to his woes.

And listen Miss Blossom did, if swishing her tail could be counted as listening. The more he talked, the more indignant he became and the faster the mare's tail swished. 'Rotten kid, judge and jury, no facts, just blame Joe O'Brien for everything that goes wrong.'

At the height of his rage he decided that if Clive could ride Miss Blossom bareback, so could he.

He climbed the fence and silently crossed the paddock to Miss Blossom. He stood on the mare's left side, just as he had seen Clive do, reached up and grasped a handful of her silvery silken mane. With a mighty spring he leapt up for her back. The leap was not good enough and he dropped back to the ground. If Clive can do it, so can I, he told himself fiercely and tried again. This time he threw one leg up at the same time, aiming it at her back. It didn't work either.

Intent as he was on conquering what seemed to be another ascent of Mount Everest, he forgot for the moment the wily character of the horse. Miss Blossom continued to graze, but her ears twitched. Eventually with a combination of jumping and climbing Joe sat upright on the mare's back, both hands wound in the mane. There was nothing to it!

Miss Blossom stopped grazing and lifted her head. Joe felt the muscled power under him and settled himself more firmly. He would trot the mare once around the pasture and then –

Miss Blossom turned her head to regard her passenger thoughtfully. Her lip curled and her teeth showed. 'Nice lady,' Joe said dutifully, giving her sides a dig with his heels, just as Clive had done. The mare didn't move. 'Beautiful lady,' he enlarged promptly.

Joe felt the muscles beneath him gather and tense. He waited in anticipation for the ride to begin.

A breathless moment passed. Miss Blossom hardly seemed to make any effort at all but she gave a curious twisting motion, and without warning Joe sailed through the air. Blue sky, white clouds, green trees revolved lazily around him.

'I should've known,' he thought in self-disgust as he prepared to land. He came down with a thump on all fours. The mare pranced across the paddock, neighed and returned to grazing.

There was a loud giggle from beyond the fence. 'Too bad, Joe,' came Vicky's piping voice. 'Miss Blossom is very partikkler who rides her. Very partikkler.'

He set his mouth. 'I want a ride now.'

'I wouldn't bother, you'll never catch her. Maybe when she knows you better, she'll give you a ride.'

He looked into the sympathetic little face that was trying hard not to laugh again and knew that she was right. He could have pounded the ground in frustration.

Not only did Clive believe that he had stolen Louisa's money, but he couldn't even ride a stupid horse!

He came to his feet and stamped away. 'Where're you going, Joe?' called Vicky. 'Can I come, too?'

'Stay away from me,' he snarled over his shoulder.

As soon as he said it, he wished that he had not, but he didn't apologise. He hid himself all afternoon and only came out when called for tea.

5

Everyone was asleep and the house was quiet. Joe had listened to the old wood creak as the house cooled after the day's heat, but now even that had finished. In the dark he glared up at the bedroom ceiling. He thought of his attempt to help Clive with the race and the rebuff he had earned for his trouble. And the contempt! A sneak thief, Clive had called him.

And the trip into town today . . . Time after time he had held his tongue instead of throwing some cutting remark at Clive. Had Clive appreciated it? He had not! He had followed him to the sweet counter in Woolies, suspicious, untrusting. Joe turned to glare at the sleeping figure in the other bed.

And when they were back home Clive had waded into him, and it had been all Clive's fault that he had butted him in the stomach. Clive had all but forced him to do it because he had shaken him, like a mouse in a cat's mouth. That had been the last straw!

This place was altogether too much to bear. He hadn't wanted to come, hadn't liked it when he arrived – nutty people with their stupid horse that threw you when you tried to ride her! He'd had it – up to his eyes. Nobody cared about him, not his social worker who'd landed him in this mess, or the Mallorys, or the dumb horse that sneered at him and wouldn't make friends – only Dad cared and he wasn't around.

Joe sat up. The answer to his misery was clear. He would leave.

He rested his chin on his hand and put his lively mind to work. Okay, he wanted out. And there was no time like the present for going. He had his pocket money, plenty to get him back to the city and home. Some would be left over for food, not enough to last until Dad came back, but he'd worry about that later.

With a glance at his sleeping room-mate Joe got up and dressed quietly. He took his zip bag from under the bed and stuffed it with clothes. All the geranium cuttings would not fit into the bag, but he managed to nest three among the clothes.

He checked that his wallet was in his jacket pocket and gave a final look around the bedroom. Goodbye and good riddance!

He slipped along the hall, down the stairs and let himself out the back door. This was more like it. It felt good to be on the move, he thought triumphantly as he latched the garden gate behind him and started along the lane. By tomorrow he would forget that he had ever been at Windrush Farm. And if he ever wanted to see a horse again – which he would not because they were daft creatures – he would go to the race course and watch the gee-gees run.

The night was warm and clear. An owl swooped low overhead on a hunt. Joe wondered if it could be one that visited the barn for mice. Louisa said there was a baby in the owl nest, still being fed by its parents. He shook his head angrily. What did he care any more about owls and barns?

No car passed as he trudged along the narrow lane with his bag in his hand. He reached the crossroads and considered waiting for the first bus into town. It would be hours yet, and he decided against it. He would walk. The lights of a lorry appeared in the distance and he stepped off the road into the shadows until it passed.

This was like old times. On his own, his own master, not at the beck and call of people who only wanted to use him to feed chickens and water a stupid horse. He reached the town an hour later, settled down on a platform bench in the station and boarded the first train into the city.

Some time later he was unlocking the front door of the O'Brien flat. The next door neighbour opened her door to take in the milk.

'Why Joe! This is a surprise,' she exclaimed. Her bottle-blonde hair was in curlers and she wore an old dressing gown. 'Home for good?' she added curiously.

'Yeah.'

'Your dad finished his spell of porridge?'

He squirmed a little. He could lie but lies led to more trouble. 'Not yet,' he answered, 'I'm sort of getting things ready for when he comes back. Don't say anything to anybody, will you?'

The woman nodded. 'Like that, is it? Well, mum's the word.' She closed the door, not wanting to be involved further.

The flat felt damp and stuffy. He opened the windows and set the cuttings in the sun. Nothing had changed since the day his social worker had collected him. Newspapers littered the couch, dirty dishes were on the table, beds unmade. He was hungry. At the farm they would be sitting down to one of Mrs. Mallory's big breakfasts, but what did that matter when he was well out of it? He opened the fridge door and his nose wrinkled in distaste at the smell. Everything inside had gone off.

Joe breakfasted on a tin of baked beans and cleaned out the fridge as he had seen Mrs. Mallory do. He decided to go the whole way and tidy the flat. Then it was time to go out to his beloved city.

Two of his pals were skateboarding on the long path by the railroad tracks. 'Hi,' said Joe coolly as they caught sight of him.

'Fingers! What's up? You're back in a hurry.' They looked glad to see him.

'Had enough.'

'Tough out there in the country, eh?' they sympathized. 'Bet they don't know about anything but cutting hay.'

Joe found himself wanting to put his pals right. Mr. Mallory knew a lot about all sorts of things, history and politics and economics, but it didn't matter now so let them think what they wanted. 'Something like that. Where's everybody?'

'Around. The Sheik's got a new girlfriend – ' The Sheik was dark and handsome but dumb as they came.

'So what else is new? What about Rikki?' Rikki was as sharp as anything, and he spent more time out of school than in.

An aircraft roared overhead, heading for the airport, and they waited until the noise level dropped. 'He's in the arcade.' Rikki liked to play the sci-fi games in the amusement arcade. 'Big Mike's with him.'

Joe's ears pricked up. Big Mike was sixteen and looking for a job now that school was finished. It seemed that he hadn't found one, but then Big Mike was not known for pushing things. He was cool, really cool. Joe had admired him ever since he came into the neighbourhood.

'Think I'll see what's happening. See you later.'

Joe ambled toward the High Street, hands in his pockets, feeling great. Old times. Nothing like 'em.

Big Mike and Rikki were between games, drinking cokes when Joe slithered through the crowded arcade and joined them. Nearby there were coloured lights flashing from the machines, exploding sounds from hits against Martian starships and moans from the players when they missed.

'Well, look who's back in town.' Rikki flashed him an amused look. Big Mike looked bored.

It was strange but Big Mike reminded him of Kip Mallory. They were about the same age, both big builds, light brown hair and eyes, but there the resemblance ended. Kip always had a keen look about him, like he was interested in everything that was happening. Big Mike looked kind of blank.

Big Mike finished off his coke and said, 'You owe me a quid, Fingers. I don't like kids scarpering without paying their debts.'

Joe blushed. 'Sorry. I forgot about it, what with everything happening at once.' He dug a handful of change from his pocket and passed over a pound coin.

Big Mike caught his wrist in a hard grasp and squeezed. Joe winced from the pain. He looked up in shock. Big Mike forced open his fist and took another pound coin.

'Hey!' protested Joe.

Big Mike sent him a long look. 'Teach you to remember.'

Rikki's smile faded. 'Come on, man, he's only a kid.'

Big Mike also sent his mate a long look. 'What'd you say?'

Rikki shrugged. 'Nothin', man. So long, Fingers,' he said pointedly.

Joe backed away and slipped out through the crowd. Some start! he thought, glum with disappointment. He could have eaten for days off that pound coin.

He wandered along the pavement, glancing in the shop windows. It was hot and the exhaust fumes from the traffic hit the back of his throat. An ambulance tore by, siren loud. He thought about an ice cream. He didn't have the money to spare to buy an ice cream, but he could steal one in a flash. He looked through the open door of a sweet shop at the freezer full of brightly wrapped ice creams asking to be nicked. He stared a long time before turning away and heading for home. Who needed ice cream? He would make himself a lemon squash with lots of ice cubes.

Joe walked up the stairs of the block of flats to his floor and saw Mr. Mallory at the front door of the O'Brien flat.

Joe gaped. Mr. Mallory said, 'Hello. A long climb up

here to the fifth floor. The lift doesn't work.'

'It doesn't more often than it does.'

Joe wondered whether he should run. He had never considered that somebody might come after him. His social worker in due course would have come by, but Joe had been prepared not to answer the door to him. His social worker would have gone away, but clearly Mr. Mallory had no such intention.

Mr. Mallory said pleasantly, 'May I come in?'

'I guess.' Joe unlocked the door and was suddenly glad that he had tidied before going out.

They went inside and Joe closed the door. 'Well,' said Mr. Mallory, choosing Dad's favourite chair and sitting down. 'Nice place you and your dad have here.'

Joe looked at the broken down couch and knew it wasn't. 'Not much but we like it.'

'Home is where the heart is, Joe, no matter what the furniture looks like. Mrs. Mallory and I hoped that you'd found a home with us, a temporary one of course until your dad is back, but a home for all that.' His open weather-beaten face was questioning.

Joe searched for something to say. 'I know.'

'We thought you were happy with us. Not much like the city but good in its own way.'

'Yes, sir.'

'Problems, were there?'

Joe scuffed the worn carpet, his mind churning at the unexpected turn of events. He was so hungry that he ached. From the open green space below the windows some kids were squealing while they played. Before long their mums would shout for them to go in to dinner.

Joe burst out, 'I didn't take Louisa's money!'

Mr. Mallory's bushy eyebrows rose nearly to his hairline. 'Nobody said you did.'

'Clive thinks I did.' Joe scuffed harder at the carpet.

'Louisa is forever misplacing her money. Clive knows that as well as the rest of us. It was wrong of him to accuse you of stealing it. Why would he think such a thing?' He waited patiently.

Joe's spirits dropped another foot. Mr. Mallory clearly didn't know that Joe O'Brien was a sneak thief, and now it was all going to come out, and of all the things that he least wanted, it was Mr. Mallory knowing.

He brushed fiercely at his eyes. 'Clive knows that – that sometimes I take sweets,' he muttered.

'And so he assumed that you took the money,' Mr. Mallory replied easily.

'I guess.'

'But we know you didn't.'

'Yes!' It was nearly a shout.

'And you were angry about it and you left.'

Joe nodded.

'I can understand now how it happened. I'm only sorry that you didn't come to me for help. That's what I'm here for. I don't pretend to be a father to you, that wouldn't be fair to your own dad, but I want to help while he's away.'

'In prison,' Joe said defiantly.

'In prison,' agreed Mr. Mallory. 'But that's hardly your fault. I'm sure your dad is proud of you.'

'And I'm proud of him. I'm going to be a pickpocket just like him when I grow up.'

To Mr. Mallory's credit he didn't blink an eye. 'Stealing is wrong, Joe. There are other ways to make him proud of you. You're a clever lad and you do well at school from what I've heard. You could be anything you want.'

Joe didn't answer. How could he explain that his dad *wanted* him to be a pickpocket, that he *expected* Joe to follow in his footsteps?

'How about it, Joe, coming back with me?'

He scowled at the ragged patch in the carpet. 'Not my scene.'

'Be honest with yourself,' Mr. Mallory said quietly.

'Do you really dislike it?'

After a long pause he admitted, 'Maybe it's not so bad.'

'We like you. It's not the same without you.'

Go back to the farm? Where owls hunted mice in the barn? And a beautiful horse lived? And kids swam in the river and played in the garden? Joe's resolve never to return wavered.

Kip would never deliberately hurt him as Big Mike had done. He had liked Big Mike! Might have continued to if he had not met Kip and learned the difference between good strength and bad strength. But Clive was at the farm and Clive scorned him. A small voice inside reminded him that Clive also praised him and laughed a lot and was fun to be with.

He glanced at his foster-father, waiting patiently for his answer. A memory nagged him, something important. 'Mr. Mallory, weren't you supposed to go to a meeting this morning?'

'Yes, I was.'

'But you came here instead?'

He looked surprised. 'Of course I did. We were worried about you.'

Joe made up his mind. 'Yes, sir, I'll go back.'

Mr. Mallory came to his feet and smiled. 'Good. I'll help you lock up the flat.'

Half an hour later they left with Joe carrying his zip bag, the geranium cuttings once again nested inside. On the way to the car they passed a hamburger bar.

Mr. Mallory stopped. 'You know, I forgot about lunch. Shall we eat here? Could you manage a hamburger, Joe?'

'I believe I could.'

He ate two cheeseburgers, a large order of french fries and a milk shake.

6

Windrush Farm had not changed, Joe discovered to his unaccountable relief as Mr. Mallory braked the car in front of the garage. Somehow he had thought that it might have, given that he had turned his back on it last night, but the house, the barn and outbuildings looked the same. Mrs. Mallory came from the house and looked warmly at her husband before hugging Joe and telling him that she was happy to see him and didn't he want a snack after the car trip?

Louisa and Clive appeared. Louisa bounced with pleasure. She said in a hearty voice, 'Knew you'd come back. Dirty, scruffy places, cities – not clean and open like here. Guess what? I found my money. I put it in the toe of my trainers yesterday and forgot about it until I put them on this afternoon.'

Mr. Mallory nodded. 'I thought it was something like that. You'd save yourself a lot of bother, poppet, if you'd use a bank.'

Joe looked distantly at Clive, and Clive's face suffused with colour.

Vicky reported to the kittens in her pocket that Joe was back and he didn't look cross any more. Joe winced when he heard her. More than ever he wished that he had not taken out his black mood on her.

Kip was still away visiting friends, and the family gathering at the evening meal was smaller than usual. Later when Joe returned to the bedroom after showering, Clive squared his shoulders and said, 'Okay, I was wrong.'

'About what?' returned Joe indifferently. He knew

very well but he would not help Clive. Clive had said that he never wanted his help again, and he would not get it. So it was with considerable surprise that he heard himself exclaim indignantly, 'I never even saw Louisa's money! I never knew where she hid it!'

'I know that now.'

Clive kicked at a chair leg and looked so downhearted that Joe was moved to say, 'About yesterday in Woolies . . . What do I owe you?'

'That's okay.'

'I get pocket money, I can afford to buy my own sweets. How much?' Clive told him, and he gave him the money.

Clive looked into the distance. 'Mike Andrews fell off his bike and dislocated his shoulder this morning.'

'Tough.' Mike Andrews was always falling off his bike, but this was the first time he had been damaged.

'Arty lost fifty pence,' Clive went on with the news of their friends.

Arty was always losing money. You'd think that he had so much he could afford to be careless. 'Arty has a screw loose.'

'Or holes in his pockets.'

They exchanged knowing grins.

There was a long silence while Clive said his prayers and Joe watched. Clive was wicket, really, he thought, using the newest term for excellence. Kind of innocent sometimes, like he didn't know which way was up, but he was as straight as they came.

Joe went to his zip bag and drew out the chocolate that he had stolen from the Village Pantry the second day he was at the farm, the theft that had passed unnoticed.

When Clive finished his prayers, Joe held up the chocolate. He cleared his throat a few times before he could say, 'You never saw me take it. It belongs to Mr. Dawson at the village shop. I couldn't eat it after you told me about him being wounded in the war and all.' He held his breath and wondered if he would have to wrestle with Clive again.

However, Clive just looked at the chocolate and rubbed his jaw. He didn't shout or anything but stood there, thinking. Joe almost sighed in relief.

'You'll have to pay for it, Joe, and apologise. I'll come with you if it'd make it easier.'

Joe admitted his most secret fear. 'Will I go up before the magistrate?' It occurred to him to wonder if his dad had this same bad feeling when he thought about being arrested. He reckoned that he did. Dad didn't like being separated from him any more than he liked being separated from Dad.

'Depends if you can convince Mr. Dawson you mean to give up thieving. If you want,' he added a little shyly, 'I'll give you a hand asking for God's help. You do want to give up stealing, don't you?'

Give up? No, he didn't want to give up! It was the way he was learning to follow in his dad's footsteps.

'Maybe,' Joe replied slowly, playing for time.

'Not good enough. You have to want to. If you can't convince yourself, how can you convince God or Mr. Dawson? And stealing's wrong, you know that as well as I do.'

Joe bit his lip, preferring to forget that particular one of the Ten Commandments. 'Do you like me?'

Clive pursed his lips at the unexpected question. 'You're great when you aren't stealing.'

That shook Joe down to his toes. He wanted Clive to like him all the time, and everybody else come to that. Deep inside he liked Clive better than anyone he'd known. You could trust him like you could trust all the Mallorys. Sure he and Clive had gone a few rounds, but all the same Clive was tops and now that he was over being cross with him, he could admit it. Everybody liked Clive – except Al Bailey who didn't count because Al was a twit –

He wanted to be like Clive, and Clive would no more steal than he would turn Miss Blossom into steaks for the table. But . . .

Joe said, 'Listen, you want to be a farmer like your dad, so you can understand. Well, I want to be like *my* dad because he's terrific. He laughs a lot and he takes me places, and we're always together, nearly always, that is,' he corrected, thinking of their present separation. 'Dad's proud of me, just like your dad is. He thinks I'll make the best pickpocket ever, and I want to live up to that.'

Clive gulped. 'But that's big trouble!'

Clive cared and that felt good.

'Joe, you've got a problem the size of a mountain, and there's only one thing for it. We'll have to ask God's help to solve it.'

'How?' replied Joe at a loss.

'Talk to God like you would anybody who's ready to help if you ask.' Clive went down on his knees, closed his eyes and got busy.

Joe blinked a bit, looked helplessly around the familiar room with its plain furniture, posters on the wall and bright curtains and finally joined him beside the bed, closing his eyes, too.

'God, sir,' Joe began in silence, 'I don't know much about this praying business, but here goes. First off, thanks for the Mallorys, they're great, and the farm's a pretty good place, too quiet and not much goes on, but there's worse places to be. The truth is, I'm glad to be back.'

He took a deep breath and plunged in. 'Secondly, I've got a problem and I can't handle it by myself.' He explained about his dad's making a living by picking pockets. 'I love my dad and I don't want to hurt him, but the truth is that I want to be more like Clive. So you see, I'm stuck. I'd be really grateful if you could give me a hand to sort it out. Amen.'

He climbed into bed wondering if he had done the job properly but somehow feeling easier.

It was after midnight when he awoke to the sound of the ghostly convoy in the lane. For a change Louisa wasn't snoring next door and he was inclined to roll over and go back to sleep, but then he recalled the strangeness of a car travelling without lights and how he and Clive had been unable to explain it. He threw back the covers and hurried to the window.

There were fewer than usual clouds in the sky, and the moonlight shone fitfully on the countryside. He had an idea. Beside the tray of flower cuttings he found a pencil stub and a scrap of paper and took them to the window. The convoy was in sight, leaving the copse of oaks where the lane ran through. He peered hard first at the sky and then the lane. With luck the moon would clear the clouds in time to see the licence plate. He waited, pencil poised.

It happened as he hoped it would. The moonlight lit the Land Rover as it passed the farmhouse and he could see the licence plate, but it proved to be muddy like the rest of the vehicle. Too muddy? No, a few letters showed, a number – he scribbled down what he could see – it would have to do.

He scrambled back into bed wondering why he had taken the trouble. What would he do with the information now that he had it? It suddenly seemed a waste of time, but all the same he put the paper safely away in the drawer of the bedside table before he went back to sleep.

Joe awoke next morning feeling hot and cold at the thought of facing Mr. Dawson, owner of The Village Pantry. Clive seemed to sense his worry because he stayed close to him until the chores were done and breakfast eaten. Then they mounted the bicycles and rode into the village.

Mr. Dawson's shop was open for the day. He kept

long hours, as long as the hours of the farming community which he served.

Mr. Dawson limped badly as he moved about the empty shop. He was a big man, heavy broad shoulders and an angled face. He would have made a fine looking Marine, Joe realised despite the sick feeling in his stomach and his quivering nerves.

Clive nodded encouragingly and Joe cleared his throat. It felt tight and dry, and it was an effort to speak. 'Mr. Dawson – ' He placed the chocolate on the counter. 'Mr. Dawson,' he began again and his voice sounded weak, like he felt.

Clive prompted him. 'Joe has something to tell you, and he's finding it hard work.'

Joe nodded. It was harder than anything he had ever done. Please God, he heard his mind say, help me!

Mr. Dawson raised an eyebrow enquiringly. 'Something wrong, Joe?' Joe nodded. 'Something about this?' He touched the chocolate and Joe nodded again.

Joe said, 'I stole it. I'm sorry. I want to pay for it.' That seemed to cover everything.

Mr. Dawson looked a little shaken. 'I see.'

'Are you going to call the police?'

Mr. Dawson thought about it while Joe's face turned red and white but he stood his ground, Clive's shoulder hard against his. 'D'you want me to?'

'No!' replied Joe with heartfelt sincerity. 'I won't do it again.' That much was true. He would never steal from the veteran again. As for anybody else – that was still unclear.

'It took considerable courage to tell me, Joe. I'll consider the matter closed.'

Joe handed over the money with an unsteady hand, but he felt good all the same and Clive looked pleased as he could be. Abruptly he understood that he had one more thing to do. 'Mr. Dawson, I want to make it up with more than money. I'd like to help you in the shop, maybe hump boxes or fill shelves. I'm a good worker and you look like you've a lot to do this morning.' There were stacks of unopened cartons on the floor.

Mr. Dawson studied him carefully and then smiled. 'You're on.'

Clive insisted on helping and together they cleared the delivery of groceries by noon. Joe whistled and sang all the way back to the farm.

That afternoon Vicky had her friends to tea. Joe heard them from the bedroom and put aside the book on magic tricks that he had borrowed from the library in town. He liked the kid and wished that he hadn't taken out his bad temper on her when he fell off Miss Blossom. Vicky didn't pester or whine like some kids did. He thought a while, gathered together a few things and went downstairs to the garden.

Vicky and her playmates were dressing up the kittens in dolls' clothes. The little girl next to Vicky seemed more intent on tying a kitten's leg in knots. Vicky looked about ready to cry.

She said, 'Grace, don't do that.'

Grace? What a name for a brat! Joe nearly laughed aloud. Grace curled her lip at Vicky and looked like Miss Blossom in her worst moments.

Joe smothered another laugh with a cough and settled beside them. Grace studied him with suspicious eyes.

'Hello, Joe. Joe's my friend,' Vicky explained to everyone with relief, sensing that help was at hand.

Joe nodded. 'Vicky, why do you have a penny behind your ear?' He asked solemnly.

Little heads swerved to stare at Vicky. 'There's no penny,' came the unanimous reply.

'Stupid,' muttered Grace.

Joe eyed her pleasantly. Here was a kid who had probably gnawed her way through her pram harness and then gone on to tear the pram apart with her baby fists.

'No?' questioned Joe. 'Then what's this?' He reached

across, took a penny from behind Vicky's small ear and held it up. The others squealed in delight. The brat sulked. Vicky stared at the coin between his fingers, rubbed her ear and smiled.

Joe smiled, too, before plucking a penny from behind the ear of each little girl in the circle, including Grace who tried to bite his hand. They demanded more, and he repeated the trick with the cut string. Vicky pressed her lips together and giggled, knowing the secret of how it was done but not telling.

There were other tricks that he had polished to perfection and he performed them all. Mrs. Mallory and the other mothers came from the house to watch, drawn by the excited cries, and later one of them asked him to entertain at a birthday party. Joe accepted after making sure that the woman was not Grace's mum.

A few days later, scrubbed and tidy, Joe entertained a dozen youngsters half his age at a farm on the other side of the village.

'They liked me,' he said afterwards when Mr. Mallory asked how it had gone. 'And I liked doing it.' He looked down at his hands wonderingly. The brat had been present but even she had eventually entered into the fun. Joe counted it as a major victory. 'The tricks were dead easy but the kids thought I was – was – '

'A magician?'

Joe grinned. 'Yes, sir, a real magician.'

'Maybe you are, lad.' Mr. Mallory clapped him on the shoulder. 'Mrs. Mallory says you're a wonder with your cups and coloured handkerchiefs. You have good, clever hands, Joe. Use them well. God doesn't give his gifts lightly.'

Joe returned to the house in deep thought.

7

'You're rich,' Clive said. He sat on the bed and watched Joe count his savings.

With his pocket money and the money which he had earned at the birthday party it seemed a lot, but Joe knew better. He had handled the O'Briens' finances too long to be excited by what might look like a small fortune. At home the O'Briens' money soon went on keeping the flat going and putting some aside for the times when Dad's luck was out. Common sense told him that his savings would soon go.

Joe gathered up the money. 'Let's go into town. My dad's birthday's coming up.'

'What're you getting him?' Clive asked later as the bus manoeuvred the narrow lanes that led to the nearby town.

'A book on house plants. Dad has a green thumb, he can make anything grow. You should've seen our flat! Looked like a greenhouse, and he was always doctoring plants people brought him. "Ask Mr. O'Brien to have a look at it" they'd say if somebody had a wonky plant. Nothing's too much trouble for my dad when it comes to growing things.'

He looked out of the window to hide the sudden sadness that he felt. He missed Dad something terrible at times like this. Watching the Mallory kids and their dad didn't help either. In fact last night with all of them in the living room together and Mrs. Mallory reading a bit from the Bible, they all looked so – so happy – that afterwards he had written a letter to Dad.

He had told him about the magic tricks he practised

and the birthday party where he had entertained and everything else that he was doing. At the end of the letter he had added a PS, almost without knowing it. He had written, 'Please, Dad, could we be the good guys for a change?'

Joe returned to the present when a sixth sense of danger kicked at his insides. He glanced around the half-empty bus. Housewives on their way to town, kids, farm workers, just what you would expect to see on a summer afternoon in the country. Why then did he feel that something was wrong?

Clive was talking to a man across the aisle. Joe looked at their fellow passenger and his eyes narrowed. This was the reason that his nerves were working overtime. He didn't like the look of the man, not at all, and he was not sure why. The man looked all right, clean shirt, buttons all there, but there was something strange about his expression, like he was excited or had a secret . . . Joe shivered and listened hard.

'Going into town for the afternoon?' the man was saying, smiling and nodding like anything.

Clive said, 'Yes, sir, my friend's looking for a present.'

Joe kicked his ankle and Clive turned in surprise. Joe sent him a warning look.

The man said, 'Hot day, maybe you boys could use an ice cream when we get into town? I know a good place, you'll like it.'

The hairs on Joe's neck lifted. Before Clive could say another word, Joe answered easily, 'We could use some ice cream all right, and when we meet our dads off the bus, that's what we'll do first.' Clive was staring at him in bewilderment. Joe ignored him and pressed on. 'My dad's a commando, his dad's a copper. They've been friends for years.'

The man's face closed up tight. He muttered something and turned away.

Clive was scandalised. He whispered to Joe, 'You lied!'

'You bet I did,' muttered Joe. 'I don't trust him an inch. I think he's one of those loonies who goes after kids.'

'He looks all right to me,' Clive protested softly.

'Not to me and I don't take chances. A lot of rotten eggs around. Al pushed you out of the race, remember? He was a rotten egg, too. If you want to pray for rotten eggs, that's fine, but meantime keep an eye on them.'

'Talk about suspicious . . .'

'Didn't your mum read from the Bible last night about Jesus sending out the twelve disciples to preach and heal? He told them they were like sheep going into a pack of wolves, and they had to be cautious as snakes and gentle as doves. That sounds like good advice to me,' finished street-wise Joe.

When the bus reached town the man hurried off and away without a word. Clive noticed and winced. 'I think you were right.'

The book was bought, wrapped with paper and string brought from the farm, and posted. Joe hoped that his dad would not find the words too hard.

They went for ice creams, polished them off in minutes and sat back and groaned in contentment. Outside the sunlight bounced off the pavements. A fine sheen of perspiration filmed Clive's forehead, and he wiped it away with the back of his hand. He looked around the snack bar at the other kids in shorts and T-shirts. 'I wish it would always be like this.'

'Yeah,' said Joe, covering a burp.

'Sun, ice cream, swimming – '

'No school.'

'Don't mention it,' Clive moaned.

'Okay, I won't mention school again.'

'You just did!'

'Sorry.' They exchanged comfortable grins.

'I don't know what to do about Al,' Clive said abruptly with a frown. 'He'll be in my year.'

'I know. He's been away all summer but he'll be back in time for the new term.'

'What're you going to do when you see him again?'

Joe considered the matter at length. Al would still be on a low boil about the race. His type would conveniently forget that he had been wrong to cheat; he'd only remember that he'd been found out. Al would be better off forgetting the whole thing and starting again from scratch, but it seemed unlikely that he would.

Joe screwed up his paper napkin and tossed it on the table. 'Before I met your lot, I'd have said "thump him before he thumps me", but now I guess I'll try to make friends with the twit. He can't have any if he goes around pushing people off race tracks.'

Clive laughed. 'There's that. Kip says that Al's brother is a first-class cricketer.'

'Yeah.'

'Maybe it's hard living up to an older brother who's a genius.'

'I guess.'

'Maybe Al's not so bad when you get to know him.'

'Let's hope so, but either way we'll have to find out. I'll have enough on my plate in a new school without dodging him.' Joe picked up the bill and took out his money.

'We'll think of something. Two great brains should come up with an answer.'

Clive sounded surer than Joe felt. 'Come on, it's time for the bus.'

It was funny how you could get used to things, Joe pondered as he soaped himself under the shower that night. When he first came to the farm he had found it really hard to get to sleep with all the quiet. Now – he paused to yawn deeply – now he could hardly wait to collapse into bed.

A loud knock came at the bathroom door, and Louisa called in exasperation, 'You goin' to be all night?'

'Probably,' he shouted cheerfully.

'Don't get smart, Joe. You're asking for a couple of frogs in your bed.'

'Croaking would make a change from your snores,' he countered, but all the same he hurried. Louisa was capable of putting frogs in his bed or slugs or anything else – she was absolutely fearless when it came to handling slimy creatures.

When Joe came out Louisa levered herself away from the wall. 'At last!'

He gave her a cheeky grin and went into the bedroom. Clive put aside his Bible, and they knelt down to say their prayers.

Joe had not come up with a solution to his problem and although God didn't seem to be rushing to help, the way things stood God remained his only hope in sorting out the muddle.

And there was another reason why he had taken to praying with Clive. Somehow he felt better when he had talked through his day with God. Things became clearer, annoyances smoothed themselves out and the good things became more important. Like the telephone call today, asking him to entertain at another children's birthday party next week.

When they finished Joe tumbled into bed, turned out the light and fell promptly asleep.

Because he did, he didn't hear the mysterious midnight traveller pass by later.

One of Joe's early morning chores was to carry buckets of fresh water to the paddock for Miss Blossom's trough. This did not endear him to the mare, but at least she had come to accept that Joe's appearance did not require instant suspicion and a baring of her large teeth. Joe decided that this was progress of a sort and talked to her with particular flattery. In return Miss Blossom allowed her long sleek neck to be stroked.

The morning that the world fell apart for the Mallory household began with Joe's journey from the water tap in the yard through the orchard to the paddock gate. He unlatched the gate, carried the buckets inside and re-latched the gate. As usual he emptied the trough of the previous day's water, scrubbed out the mud and leaves with a handful of grass and poured in the fresh water. At this point he grew uneasy.

In the past few days Miss Blossom had taken to watching this routine from a position beyond Joe's left shoulder. It may have been that Joe fed her an apple from the orchard when he finished his job, but he liked to think that Miss Blossom was being friendly.

This morning as he worked he became aware that he didn't hear her. He looked around and saw that she was not at his shoulder.

He straightened up to shade his eyes against the light and looked around the fenced paddock. Miss Blossom was nowhere to be seen. Disbelieving his eyes, Joe checked again but the silk-coated mare was not in sight.

Joe frowned. 'Come out, you nuisance,' which he admitted to himself was a silly thing to say because apart from a few trees there was no place for a horse to hide.

He didn't like it. Not a bit. He picked up the empty buckets, tore back to the farmyard and found Mr. Mallory.

'She's not there!' he said incredulously.

Mr. Mallory looked up from his work. 'Who's not there?'

'Miss Blossom. I took her fresh water, and she's not in the paddock.'

Mr. Mallory stood up, wiped his hands on his trousers and said, 'Let's have a look.'

Joe ran back, Mr. Mallory hurried after him. The paddock remained empty.

Mr. Mallory stood at the fence and gripped the top rail until his knuckles whitened. Joe felt a great dread creep into his bones. Clearly Mr. Mallory had no idea where Miss Blossom had gone.

Joe said numbly, 'The gate was latched when I came. She couldn't have got out by herself.'

Without a word Mr. Mallory returned to the house and called everyone together. Mrs. Mallory, Clive, Joe, Louisa, Vicky and the two farmworkers gathered in the living room while he organised a search of the entire farm from the river to the farthest field.

'She must be somewhere,' he said. 'Joe assures me that the gate was latched when he took her water, and I accept it. She must have jumped the fence.'

Louisa's eyes darkened. She knew as well as Joe that Miss Blossom was too lazy for high jinks.

'Search carefully and be back here in an hour.'

Joe and Clive exchanged careful looks and went their ways.

An hour later they were back. The others drifted in. There was no sign of the missing horse.

Vicky began to whimper and Mrs. Mallory took her into the kitchen to start breakfast. Mr. Mallory picked up the phone and dialled. No one asked who he was calling. They all knew that the police would have to take over.

Joe and Clive returned to their chores. They might be worried sick about Miss Blossom but pets and animals depended on them and had to be fed.

Clive said, 'We'd better let Kip know. Miss Blossom was bought for him when he started school. He thinks the world of her.'

'The police will find her,' Joe said stoutly.

Some time later Joe examined what he had said and found it strange. All his life he had looked on the law as the enemy, just like his dad did. Yet here he was, staring at the lane in front of the farmhouse, willing a thousand Panda cars to roar up to a screeching halt and a thousand policemen to leap out and begin the search for a beautiful, vain, stubborn, bad-tempered horse.

In fact Police Constable Jim Gough arrived on his bicycle. PC Gough lived at the edge of the village and his house also served as a police station. Joe had seen Mrs. Gough hanging out washing in the garden. While he had not exactly sneered at this country-type arrangement for law enforcement, he had been far from impressed.

Now Joe found the constable's weather-beaten face infinitely comforting. His big solid frame seemed to take over the living room, and even Louisa cheered up. Joe snapped to attention when PC Gough questioned him.

Yes, Joe replied, he had been in the paddock first thing just as he was every day. He described what he had found – nothing – yes, the gate had definitely been latched when he arrived. And so on.

Finally the leather covered notebook was closed and the pencil replaced in the upper pocket of the uniform. Mr. Mallory walked the constable to his bicycle, and Joe and Clive watched from the front door until PC Gough pedalled back toward the village.

8

'What do you think, Joe?' Clive asked when PC Gough's bicycle was out of sight.

Mr. Mallory closed the garden gate with a weary gesture and walked toward the house. His pleasant, open face was twisted with worry.

The most terrible thought in the world leapt into Joe's mind and left him stunned and horrified.

'Joe? I said – '

'I heard you.' His voice rasped. 'Clive,' he began and then closed his eyes briefly. When he opened them Clive was staring at him. 'Clive,' he began again, 'do you remember the church picnic?'

'Course I do.'

'Do you remember when we tied up the bunting and what we heard your dad and the other men talking about?'

'Sure – ' Clive's voice died, and he turned white. He licked his lips before he said, 'Are you thinking that Miss Blossom's been stolen like those horses in the next county?'

Joe nodded carefully.

'But that means – '

Joe shook his head. 'Don't even say it.' If Clive put his worst fear into words he would run halfway to China, but the words that he had heard at the picnic were there in his mind to torment him: horse meat for the Continent. He shuddered deeply.

Clive said, 'I can't believe it.'

'Look at your dad's face. He believes it.'

Mr. Mallory joined them at the front door. Clive said

stiffly, 'Dad, what did PC Gough say to you when he was leaving?' Mr. Mallory shook his head.

Clive's shoulders slumped. 'You can tell us, Dad. I think Joe's figured it out already.'

Mr. Mallory clasped his son's shoulders. 'He couldn't be sure, of course, but he thinks she might have been stolen by the gang who's at work around here. It seems they've moved into our county now. Yes, I'm afraid he thinks Miss Blossom may already be on her way abroad.' He rubbed his berry-brown nose. 'I'd better phone Kip and let him know the latest. Your mother's going to be very upset. She chose Miss Blossom, you know.'

Afterwards Joe and Clive found a corner in the garden and talked about it over and over, as if talking would bring Miss Blossom home.

And in the torrent of words they shared, Joe thought, 'This is how people feel when they have something precious stolen! Angry, hurt, sad. This is how people feel when Dad lifts their wallets and takes their money and throws away the pictures and things they want!'

Clive was shaking his shoulder. 'You okay? You look weird.'

Joe came to his feet. 'I'm okay. Let's find something to do, I'm going spare sitting here.'

They wandered into the house. Louisa was at the dining room table with the morning post spread out around her. She looked up when they came in and her eyes were red. She held out some letters to Clive. 'These are for Mum.' He took them and went to find Mrs. Mallory.

Louisa heaved a sigh. 'I got the stuff on being an air hostess.' She had changed her mind again about her career and had written to British Airways for information. 'Care to see it?'

'No, thanks.'

She gathered the glossy leaflets together and crumpled them between her hands.

'Aren't you going to read them?'

'Not interested any more.'

Joe said, 'Will you ever make up your mind about what you want to do?'

Louisa sighed. 'Promise not to laugh?'

'Cross my heart. . . .'

'What I'd really and truly like to do is to grow things, like Dad.'

'I can understand that. My dad likes to grow things, too. It's a kind of hobby with him.' He wondered if Louisa knew what his dad did for a living. He hoped that she didn't because after what had happened that morning it hurt to think of his dad stealing anything from anybody.

Louisa said, 'That's nice.'

'So why don't you plan to go to agricultural college or something?'

She looked away. 'I feel silly about it. The girls at school laughed when I told them. They want to do something glamorous and exciting like being an air hostess.' She pushed the crumpled papers with her forefinger. 'They think I'm a wimp.'

Joe leaned his elbows on the table. 'Some friends!'

'They're okay, but they change their minds oftener than I do. They're not like you, Joe, you're so sure of yourself. I'd like to be like you.'

Joe's eyebrows soared. If Louisa could only see inside his brain where everything was going round and round! Pain about the way that Dad hurt people by stealing from them and doubt about following his dad's way of life.

He came to his feet. 'Forget what a bunch of silly girls think. Do what suits you.'

She sighed. 'You're right and I will. I'm tired of trying to be like them, but they'll laugh and I don't like being laughed at.'

'So laugh back. You know where you're headed and

they don't have a clue where they're going. You're one up.'

'You're sharp. I'd never have thought of that. Joe – do you think we'll find Miss Blossom?'

He wanted to cry out 'How do I know?' but he didn't. He said instead, 'I hope so.'

The day passed so slowly that it seemed more like a week. Each time the telephone rang, Joe's heart pounded, but PC Gough didn't call. Kip was phoned and Mrs. Mallory sniffed a lot as she told him what PC Gough had said.

By mid-afternoon the news had travelled halfway round the neighbourhood. Friends dropped by, and Clive and Joe soon had a circle of anxious faces around them. Questions flew and were answered as best as they could be. Mike Andrews' sister said that he was still in hospital with his dislocated shoulder and that two of their horses had been stolen last week and she knew just how they felt.

Finally there was nothing more to say about Miss Blossom. After a long pause someone said, 'Al's back. Saw him in town yesterday.' Joe perked to attention. 'He was still browned off about the race. Said you two had it in for him.'

'We don't,' said Clive. 'The race is water under the bridge.'

'You and Joe know it, but Al doesn't. Says he's gonna get you two before you get him.'

Clive groaned. 'Nutter!'

Joe caught his eye and signalled a silent message. Could Al have taken Miss Blossom? Clive shook his head.

Their friends trailed away to their homes and the two boys were left alone again. Clive said, 'Al lives miles away. He couldn't possibly have walked through the night to take Miss Blossom without his folks knowing.'

'Pity,' said Joe who had been hoping for a quick

solution.

'Al's a twit but he's no *thief.*' Clive was so absorbed in his own thoughts that he didn't notice Joe wince.

Clive squared his shoulders. 'When this is over – '

'And Miss Blossom's back,' interrupted Joe stoutly.

'Then we'll straighten out Al. We have to because school'll be rotten if he's out to get us.'

When Mr. Mallory finished his work he drove into the village to speak to PC Gough but came back with no further news. An all points bulletin had been issued to be on the lookout for the stolen horse, enquiries were being made – in fact everything that could be done to find Miss Blossom was being done.

That night Joe and Clive prayed hard each in his own way for her safety.

Joe did his chores next morning with his chin dragging, purposely dawdling to make up the time that he would have spent with the mare. After breakfast he stacked his dishes on the kitchen counter, drank the rest of his milk and added the empty glass. And then he remembered the licence plate number written on a scrap of paper and stored in the drawer of the bedside table.

Much later, when Joe had time to think about it, he blessed that moment. In his prayers he had asked God to look after the mare and bring her home again safely. He had also asked for God's help to be sharp-witted and to be ready for what might be needed of him. And that's exactly what had happened.

But now, while the others brushed by him, he stood stock still at the kitchen counter and thought hard about the licence number and why he had taken the trouble to copy it. Any Land Rover and horse box that travelled in the dead of night without lights just had to be suspicious! He fought down the wave of excitement that threatened to blur his thinking. And not only did it just have to be suspicious, but it could very well have something to do with the disappearance of Miss Blossom!

Joe came alive and dragged Clive outside into the garden to tell him as much. 'What can we lose by telling the local bobby what we both saw for ourselves?' he demanded.

Clive's eyes glittered. He was suddenly as excited as Joe. 'Not a thing. Let's go.'

They ran to the barn, pulled out the bicycles and pedalled furiously into the village.

The combination home and police station had a lantern-shaped light with 'Police' in white letters on the blue glass. The garden was full of flowers and an apple tree begged to be stripped of its fruit. Joe didn't see any of it. He propped his bike by the front door and rang the doorbell.

Mrs. Gough answered, drying her hands on her apron. 'Yes, boys?' Beyond her was an office with a desk, filing cabinet and pegs hung with oilskins and anoraks.

Clive almost stuttered in his haste. 'Is he here?'

'No, PC Gough has gone over to Andrews' farm, but he'll be back by noon.'

'Can we phone him? I'm Joe O'Brien and this is Clive Mallory. His horse was stolen and we think maybe we have some important information.'

'You'd better come in.'

They trooped inside. 'Do your folks know you're here?' asked Mrs Gough.

'No, Mrs Gough, we were in too much of a hurry to tell them.' Clive shifted impatiently from one foot to the other.

'I can see that.' She picked up the receiver and began dialling. Joe held his breath. 'Has PC Gough arrived yet?' she asked someone on the other end of the line. She listened. 'Yes, ask him to call the station when he comes in. Thank you.'

Joe turned to Clive in disappointment.

She put down the phone and said, 'If you write down the message, I'll give it to him when he calls.'

There was little else to do. Joe took the number from his pocket and copied it on the pad. There seemed precious little to it – a few letters, a number, but perhaps it would be enough to trace the mysterious vehicle.

Clive explained about the midnight traveller as Joe wrote. 'We didn't think much about it until Miss Blossom disappeared, but now – well, don't you think it might be important?'

Mrs. Gough would not commit herself, but she said warmly, 'I hope so. Now the two of you had better go home. My husband will phone as soon as he knows anything.'

They trundled the bicycles back to the road, mounted and rode slowly back through the village. After all the hope and expectation of the wild ride there, they felt let down.

Clive said firmly, 'It means something, I know it does.'

'You bet it does. Anybody stealing horses has to have a horse box to take them away in – '

'Or a lorry – maybe they aren't using a horse box at all,' Clive said sadly. 'Maybe they're taking them away in a lorry.'

'I never thought of that. Whatever they use has only to be big enough for a horse to stand in, and there are lots of trucks and things that would be big enough.'

'But the Land Rover and the horsebox are good bets because they're stealing them one at a time.'

'The best,' Joe said, to keep up their spirits. 'And remember – there were no lights on the ones we saw.'

'Absolutely!' They rode through the village and out the other side toward the Mallory farm, hoping that they were right.

The entrance to Oak Acres came into sight. It hadn't changed in all the time that Joe had been with the Mallorys. Still deserted, still lonely. It set him thinking all over again.

'Clive, where would you hide a stolen horse?'

'What a question!'

'Well, where would you?' Joe persisted. 'Whoever's doing this has to have a kind of headquarters where they hide the horses they steal. They wouldn't run each one to the coast and ship them one at a time. It would cost too much and they're out to make money.'

'So they'd keep them together until they had a shipment.'

'And then they'd load them up and drive them to a ship. So where would they keep them?'

Clive pondered. 'Somewhere secret where nobody'd see them.'

'Like a deserted farm?' ventured Joe.

'Like a deserted farm,' agreed Clive.

'Like Oak Acres?' The words came out in a rush.

'Are you off your nut? Oak Acres! That's practically next door to us.'

'So? Why should you notice anything wrong at Oak Acres? You're not expecting anything to be wrong, and you never go there. Why should you go there?'

'No reason, but Oak Acres! No way.'

They pedalled on until Clive pulled over to the side of the road and came to a stop. Joe pulled in beside him.

'Winkle was a ratfink,' said Clive firmly.

Joe looked at him sharply. His friend was not given to saying ill of people, in fact he was the opposite, so if he called the bankrupt owner of Oak Acres a ratfink, without a doubt he was.

Clive went on, 'Dad once came near to saying that he was a miserable old skinflint and didn't mind how he made his money. Winkle wouldn't mind renting out his empty farm to a bunch of horse rustlers, it would be just up his alley.'

'And the farm isn't up for sale yet. That's peculiar.'

'You bet it's peculiar.'

They looked at each other. 'Shall we go back and leave another message for PC Gough?'

Joe nodded soberly. 'Just what I was about to suggest.'

Mrs. Gough made no comment on the view that Oak Acres was a good place to hide stolen horses but wrote it on the pad below the licence plate number.

9

The August morning had clouded over when Clive and Joe left the village again and a breeze, soft with the scent of rain, met them head-on as they free-wheeled down a long gentle slope. The boys were too involved with their thoughts to notice.

Clive said, 'It's been thirty-six hours since Miss Blossom disappeared.'

'I know.' Joe could think of little else.

'D'you think we're clutching at straws about Winkle's place?'

Joe swerved into the verge and swung off the bike. His thin face was tight and urgent. 'We aren't because it makes sense. And something else makes sense! If Oak Acres is a good place to hide stolen horses, then maybe at this very minute Miss Blossom is there!' Joe fisted the handlebar. 'We need to look at the farm. Now.'

'Us? You and me?'

'We need to check this very minute because she's been gone thirty-six hours and she could be moved any time – if she hasn't already.'

'You're right.'

They hid their bicycles in the undergrowth, quietly discussing what they would do. No heroics or foolishness. They would simply go up to the house and see for themselves whether a farmhouse which was supposed to be empty actually was, there and back in fifteen minutes or less. If it looked as if sculduggery was afoot then they would report it on the double.

'I'll lead,' Joe said. 'I'm used to snaking my way through back alleys.'

They started up the dirt track. It didn't look as if any vehicles had passed that way for a long time, but it was easy enough to brush away tyre marks. At the first bend Joe slipped into the trees, Clive close on his heels. From there on the track would be in full view of the house and, as Joe murmured, there was no point in trumpeting their arrival.

They made their way through the trees as silently as they could until the clearing and the house came into view then slipped behind a large oak for a whispered conference.

'The garden's a shambles, weeds as high as the sills,' Joe commented. 'Great for creeping up to the house.'

'Creeping?' Clive's whisper was scandalised.

'How else do we get there without being seen? If somebody *is* there, we don't want them to know we're here.'

Since there didn't seem to be any answer to that, Clive just nodded, but sneaking went against the grain and his conscience bothered him something awful.

Joe dropped to his stomach and wriggled into the tall growth. He hoped there were no nettles. Nettles made his skin itch and burn. He chose a line that made good use of the few bushes growing above the weeds. He could hear Clive behind him, moving with all the control and neatness that Joe anticipated and that by comparison made him feel as clumsy as an elephant charging through a forest.

At the house Joe rose to his feet and peered cautiously into the front window. An empty room. He sank down again, pointed to the corner of the house and took off. A stronger breeze shivered the leaves on the trees, and for a moment he could not distinguish the different sound that reached his ears. The sound of a pop group playing.

Joe stopped and cupped his ear. Clive nodded in understanding, his mouth set hard. Joe began to wish that they had not come: this was no game in the back streets of his neighbourhood. If they were caught there would be trouble. He remembered the beautiful mare galloping across the paddock in the early morning, the sun on her champagne coloured coat, and he clenched his teeth and crept forward again. In no time a window lay ahead and above him.

He slithered up the wall, pressed his back against the rough brick and risked a glance. The window was open, and inside the room two men sat at a table playing cards. A small transistor radio played softly. Two unmade camp beds stood against the wall.

Joe stood back and listened hard. One of the men was grumbling, the one with ginger hair Joe reckoned, because he had a peevish look about him. 'Should've been here by now.'

The other man agreed. 'An hour late already. I told Winkle not to use a new driver, but no, he knew best. Best, ha! Winkle may have thought up this lark, but we did all the organising.'

'Amateurs!' declared Ginger in disgust.

'Horses're like anything else for the taking, only bigger. You gotta plan, get it all together.'

'Yeah, get it all together. Too bad Winkle's turned sour. This is a great little caper.'

'Great little caper, but he's got a point. If he waits any longer to put this place up for sale, people'll ask questions.'

A chair scraped back and someone walked across the room. Joe and Clive slithered down and hunched themselves into the smallest possible space.

Ginger's voice came from the window. 'Maybe we should bring in the gee-gees.'

'Won't take long once the transport's here. Sit down and have another hand.'

Joe signalled Clive to leave. They crawled beside the wall until they reached the back of the house and then exchanged looks of despair. Joe put his mouth to Clive's ear, 'Did you hear that? He said gee-gees, more than one horse. Miss Blossom's bound to be here, but they're ready to take her away!'

'Let's find her. Try the barn.'

Nothing stirred behind the house and they shot across the farmyard to the barn, eased open one of the big double haywain doors and slipped inside.

'Crumbs!' Clive muttered.

On a stone floor which in the old days had been used for winnowing grain free of chaff now stood a dirty Land Rover, plastered in dried mud. Behind it stood a horse box.

Joe pointed expressively and Clive nodded. The vehicles could be none other than the ones they had seen travelling in ghostly darkness through the night hours.

On both sides of the stone floor partitions had been built. Joe ran through the left-hand doorway and Clive took the right one. They both emerged from the dim cavernous areas shaking their head.

Joe wiped his streaming forehead. He felt hotter than fire in here. 'Nothing but an old cart.'

'Not even that much on my side.'

'So where's Miss Blossom?'

They checked the back of the house for signs of the two men, but there was no movement behind the uncurtained windows and the music from the transistor radio continued unbroken.

'She has to be *somewhere*,' Joe declared. 'How about a deserted quarry?'

'None around here. Let me think a minute.'

Joe clamped down on an urge to groan. Poor Miss Blossom! So near and yet so far.

But Clive didn't have his minute. The back door of the house opened and footsteps crossed the yard. From the distance came the sound of a heavy vehicle entering the track to the farmhouse. The gang's transport had arrived! Joe was sure that his heart would leap from his rib cage.

They scurried through the barn and out the double doors at the back where the haywains had left after unloading. A worn path lay to the right, and they pounded along until they were out of sight.

Joe looked at his friend in blank despair. 'What now?' he panted.

Clive didn't seem nearly so downhearted. 'There's no sign of a horse in the barn, so Miss Blossom must be outside, grazing. And since she has to be kept out of sight, she must be in a hollow or among some trees. Come on, I think I know the perfect spot.'

Joe regarded his friend with hope. 'Lead on.'

Clive set off along the path at a trot. 'Looks good,' he said. 'The path goes near those trees – you wouldn't think it from here, but there's a little clearing in there and a stream leading to the river. Kip and I explored it once.'

They left the path and struck off to the nearby copse. Clive's face lit up. 'The dead wood's been piled up between the trees like a fence. The clearing's been made into a holding pen!'

They peered over the top of the makeshift fence. Miss Blossom was quietly cropping the lush grass.

Clive said softly, 'Thank you, God.'

'Oh yes, thank you,' Joe echoed in heartfelt gratitude.

The mare was not alone. Three other horses grazed with her and each was tethered to a stake driven into the ground.

'Right,' said Clive. 'Let's get going. We each lead two.'

They scrambled and tore their way through the dead wood. Clive raced to the far side of the clearing and began untying a chestnut. Joe headed for the nearest horse which was Miss Blossom.

'Hello, beautiful lady,' Joe said. 'Glad to see me?' He

bent down and untied the tether from the stake. Miss Blossom looked on indifferently. 'It's Joe, don't you know me? That's Clive over there, and we're here to rescue you.'

Miss Blossom snorted through her velvety nose and ambled toward a fresh patch of grass. Joe pulled her after him as he bent to untie the next horse. Miss Blossom butted him in the back and he fell face down. 'Come on, give me a break for once,' Joe muttered as he picked himself up and started again.

'Miss Blossom,' Clive called sharply, 'behave yourself. No time to act like a prima donna.'

'What's a prima donna?' Joe asked lightly, taking a firm grip on both ropes. He felt great!

'The top lady singer in an opera. Sometimes they act like Miss Blossom does. Hold it!'

Both boys froze. Someone was coming along the path . . .

Joe hissed. 'Let's split.' He headed for the path.

Clive grabbed at his sleeve. 'Not that way, we'll run smack into him. There has to be another way out. A bunch like this would have a backdoor escape.'

It occurred to Joe that his friend was learning fast.

Joe's glance checked the seemingly impenetrable barrier of dead wood. 'Where?'

'God gave you good eyes, use them!'

At the far corner of the holding pen there seemed to be more brush than wood. Joe pulled the two horses after him and investigated. The fence gave way easily under his hand, and he pushed it aside. 'This way.'

Clive ran up with his two horses and they hit the escape path at Mach one, slower than the speed of light but faster than they would have believed possible. All too soon they heard a shout. 'He's discovered the horses are gone,' Clive gasped on the run.

Joe wiped his face and realised that it was raining, big fat drops that seemed to sizzle on his feverish skin.

'Maybe he'll think the horses got loose by themselves.'

'By untying their own tethers? Pull the other leg.'

'He'll be after us.'

'He is already.'

They splashed across the narrow stream and into the trees beyond. Joe's heart pounded. A V-junction appeared in the path, and Joe slid to a stop. Miss Blossom came up behind and he pushed her head away before she could nip his shoulder. Miss Blossom did not seem in the least grateful for her timely rescue.

'Hold it, Clive. I'll take the left fork and make sure he follows me. You take the horses up the right one.'

Clive called over his shoulder. 'Don't be daft. He'll follow the hoof prints, no matter what you do.'

'But he'll catch up at this rate.'

'I've got a better idea.' Clive dropped the two lead ropes he held and gave the rump of each horse a smack. They started forward.

Clive ran back to Joe and sent the third horse on its way ahead. He leapt astride Miss Blossom and reached for Joe's hand. 'Climb up, we'll ride and herd at the same time.'

Joe gritted his teeth, took the outstretched hand and somehow clambered onto Miss Blossom's back. He settled himself in front of Clive and wound his hands into the silky mane. It seemed a long way to the ground, and after his last experience astride the mare he didn't look forward to this one.

Clive's arms came around him and his hands fastened on the mane, too. 'Okay?' he asked in Joe's ear.

Joe gulped. 'Okay.' The patter of rain was stronger now and he licked his upper lip, tasting the cool moisture.

Miss Blossom set off at a lazy trot, the other horses strung out ahead of her on the narrow path. Joe began to bounce and clung tighter still, his legs straining hard against the mare's sides to hold himself in place. A limpet could not have tried to press closer to a rock. Why hadn't he asked Clive to teach him to ride bareback!

He screwed his eyes shut. 'Please God,' he prayed silently, 'don't let me fall off.'

Clive said in his ear, 'He's not coming after us.'

Joe had to force himself to remember why they were taking this crazy ride. 'Good.'

'Wrong. It's bad. He must have gone back for his mate, and they've got wheels.'

Joe swallowed hard. 'We'd better gallop or we won't get to the lane before they do.' In the lane there would be cars passing and they would be safe.

Clive called to Miss Blossom, 'Hurry up, lady,' and at the same time he kicked her sides. Miss Blossom slowed.

'What's the matter?' Joe moaned. He would never again climb more than a foot off the ground.

'She's cross. She doesn't like carrying two riders.'

Cross! Joe could have howled. Here they were, trying to save her from the butcher's block, and she was cross because she carried two riders!

Joe risked opening his eyes. Beyond Miss Blossom's pointed ears the three horses jogged along at a sedate pace. They would never race unless Miss Blossom did, and then the instinctive need to join in would take over.

Ahead was the track between Oak Acres farmhouse and the lane. The three horses rounded the corner into the track. Miss Blossom stepped daintily after them and suddenly when the lane and safety were only a matter of a few hundred metres ahead, she stopped. Dead still. Her tail swished, her ears twitched and she snorted. Clive pleaded, urging her on, telling her she was beautiful and saying all the other soppy stuff that was needed to get her to respond to his frantic kicks in her side. Miss Blossom ignored it.

Joe groaned.

Clive called, 'Please, lovely lady, *fly!*'

Miss Blossom stood her ground.

From the farmhouse farther up the track came the low smooth sound of a well-tuned car engine. Joe recognised it instantly. 'They've got the Land Rover.'

'They'll be up to us in no time. We'll run again.' Clive made to jump down but Joe held up a hand.

Joe's eyes narrowed and his face grew stern. The steady rain dripped off his nose and his shirt was wet through, but his mind was clear. It was time to stop pampering Miss Blossom.

He leaned forward and screamed in her ear. 'Ugly old cow! Ugly, ugly old cow!' Clive drew a swift breath of horror. Joe paid no attention. He screamed again. 'You're a skinny hag – with warts – great, hairy warts!'

The sound of the car engine grew louder; it was leaving the barn, crossing the farmyard and rounding the house. It would be on the track any second now and would thunder down on them. Joe angrily wiped the rain from his eyes. His idea had not worked. They would have to get down, pull Miss Blossom after them and try to make a run for it. He didn't think much of their chances.

Miss Blossom's shoulders twitched and heaved. Her iron-shod hind hoof kicked out, and the muscles in her hind quarters bunched. Something was brewing in her little pea brain! Joe thought with a rush of hope. 'Hang on,' he muttered to Clive.

Like an arrow shot from a longbow, Miss Blossom launched herself at the track ahead, head outstretched, ears erect, nostrils flared. In a frenzy of horsey anger she galloped, silver mane flowing in the wind, powerful muscles working in splendid co-ordination beneath the silky coat.

Joe wound his hands tighter still in the long mane and hung on for dear life.

'It worked!' Clive crowed in triumph.

They caught up with the other horses ambling along,

passed them as if they had been standing still and flew into the bend, mud spraying from Miss Blossom's churning hooves. The three horses instinctively began to gallop after them. Above the pounding and splashing came the sound of the car engine, effortlessly eating up the distance.

The lane was in sight; a car travelling along it passed the entrance to Oak Acres, but behind them the raucous blast of a car horn scattered the three horses. The Land Rover roared through, made up the distance and was suddenly alongside them.

Ginger waved angrily from the front seat. 'Pull over! Those horses belong to us! Stop right now!'

'In a pig's eye!' growled Clive.

Miss Blossom took exception to the noisy smelly monster beside her. She increased her speed and the lane was at hand. Clive attempted to turn her and could not. She tore across the lane, jumped the narrow drainage ditch and entered the opposite field.

The last thing that Joe and Clive saw as Miss Blossom headed home to her own paddock was a police Panda car in pursuit of a Land Rover with two irate villains inside.

10

'But where did the policeman and the Panda car come from?' Louisa enquired plaintively. She was having trouble taking in all that had happened since she had seen Joe and Clive at breakfast.

At the moment there looked to be little difference between her brother and the lad from the back streets. Both looked exhausted, their faces drawn and white beneath their tanned skins. Each pair of eyes was a mirror reflection of his friend's, but far from being tired the expression was bright with triumph.

From what Louisa had sorted out in the garbled account of the morning, she reckoned that they had every reason to feel like winners. They had figured out where Miss Blossom was held, followed it up by having a look for themselves and then, when the mare was in their grasp, they had been forced to think fast and spirit her away with the gang hot on their heels.

And not only had Miss Blossom been saved but also the two saddle horses from the Andrews Farm and Mr. Black's prize jumper. At this very minute all three were probably being collected by their owners and on their way home again.

Clive used a currycomb on Miss Blossom's mane as he answered Louisa's question. 'PC Gough called his wife when he reached the Andrews Farm, just like she asked. And then he telephoned into town for a car to go out and check Oak Acres. They arrived just as we left.'

'So really, you didn't need to go through all that?' she asked doubtfully.

'Wrong. The transport to take the horses away had

arrived, and if we hadn't stalled them, Miss Blossom and the others would be nearing the coast by now.'

Joe didn't like to be reminded of how close the whole thing had been. He put down the brush he was using on Miss Blossom's coat and drank some of the hot soup which Mrs. Mallory had brought to the barn when she saw how wet and cold they were.

Louisa had brought towels and dry clothing to the barn because neither Joe nor Clive would leave the mare until she had been rubbed down, brushed and combed. The boys had taken turns drying and dressing themselves so that the work would not stop. Miss Blossom was presently champing at something tasty in a nose bag.

The ride home from Oak Acres had been almost as wild as the ride to avoid the two men, Joe recalled with a wince and surreptitiously rubbed his sore bottom. For a lazy self-satisfied mare Miss Blossom had shown a turn of astonishing energy, flying across fields in the pouring rain, swerving and jumping ditches just as if she never spent her days in pampered laziness.

And all the time he and Clive had clung to her back, yipping and hollering with excitement and urging her on while fences and trees sped by in a blur.

Miss Blossom had headed straight for the paddock when they reached the farm, but Clive persuaded her that the barn was a more suitable place for making her pretty again. While Joe got to work with dry cloths on her coat, Clive had reported to the house. The Mallorys had immediately rushed to the barn.

Mr. Mallory had looked at the mud-spattered horse, dripping wet, and said softly, 'Welcome home, lady,' then clapped the boys on the shoulder. 'Good work, both of you.'

Mrs. Mallory had been inclined to worry over what might have happened to the boys had they not escaped, but even she put aside her forebodings in the joy of the moment. Vicky had plugged her thumb into her mouth and looked on with wide enchanted eyes.

Louisa sighed. 'Beats me how two cuckoos like you could do all that, but I'm glad you did.' She clapped her forehead, 'Kip! He's waiting for news!' and tore away to the house to phone.

It had all been highly satisfactory, thought Joe that night, and he told God all about it and remembered to thank him for strong legs. 'Otherwise I might not have lasted,' he added gratefully. Afterwards Joe and Clive talked in the dark.

Joe said, 'It wouldn't have worked if I hadn't insulted Miss Blossom, called her an ugly old cow. She knew what I was saying, all right, and did it make her boil! That was a stroke of luck.' He paused and thought it over. 'Or maybe it wasn't. I remember asking God to help me keep alert to what needed to be done and, you know, I reckon that's exactly what he did. What do you think, Clive?'

The sound of deep, even breathing was his answer. Clive had fallen asleep.

Joe could scarcely move when he awoke the next morning. His bones ached and so did muscles which he never knew he had. The insides of his legs were chafed nearly raw and as for his backside! He preferred not to imagine the bruising . . . He groaned dramatically.

Clive opened his eyes and yawned. 'Stiff?'

'Dead and don't know it.'

'Mum'll give you some liniment.'

'Should I drink it or rub it on?'

'Bathe in the stuff. You'll pong but you'll live.'

Joe stretched a little under the sheets. Even his toes ached! 'Come the day I can throw away the crutches and plaster casts, bandages and whatever I'll need to survive this, I want to learn to ride Miss Blossom. She owes me that.'

Clive turned over and winced. 'I don't feel so great

myself.' He threw aside the covers and stood up, testing various parts of his body. There were chores to be done and animals to be fed. 'Ride Miss Blossom? Of course I'll teach you, but by now I reckon you've learned by experience! A little practice should see you ready for the circus.'

Joe grinned, dragged himself from bed and dressed with care.

His body ached but his mind sailed with the clouds that day. After breakfast Mr. Andrews drove by and thanked them. His saddle horses, family pets, were safe at home with no harm done. He was a thin, small man who didn't look as if he could stay on the back of a huge horse, much less handle it with skill and mastery, which Clive assured Joe that he did.

Mr. Black arrived later, having farther to come. He looked like Mr. Mallory, big, solid, square set, hardly the type to go all soft-eyed over anything, especially a four-legged creature that spent most of its time munching grass. His horse was enormous, Joe recalled, powerful enough to carry its owner all right, but he found it difficult to picture the two of them sailing over hedges and such as he'd seen on TV. There was no accounting for people, Joe thought, with a touch of superiority until he remembered that he himself was just as peculiar. He, Joe 'Fingers' O'Brien, had fallen head over heels for a stupid horse named Miss Blossom! After that he didn't feel superior to Mr. Black, only sympathetic.

It was all great but embarrassing, too, having to sit there and listen to all the praise. Joe was frankly glad when it was over.

Before lunch PC Gough rode up on his bicycle and went over the statements that they had made the previous day when the police came by. Mrs. Gough sent her regards. The sun came out and the earth steamed gently under the hot rays.

Some days later an unfamiliar car drove along the lane, and parked in the lay-by in front of the gate. Upstairs in the bedroom Joe glanced down at it in idle curiosity but returned to working with the geraniums. The cuttings were growing nicely and, according to Mr. O'Brien's instructions which had arrived in a letter that morning, he was transplanting them into pots. There had been other news in the mis-spelt letter, and Joe had read it with pleasure: Mr. O'Brien's work in the prison vegetable garden had earned him considerable praise. His potatoes were the biggest within a hundred miles. How about that? Mr. O'Brien had finished proudly.

How about that indeed, thought Joe. It would be good to have something to brag about his dad like other kids did.

A thin lady got out of the car to be greeted by Mrs. Mallory.

A few minutes later Clive came in and closed the bedroom door behind him. 'That's Al Bailey's mother downstairs. Al's in the car. Mum says we should keep him company because he doesn't want to come in.'

The boys had all but forgotten Al in the days since Miss Blossom's return, but now the memory of the ill-fated race came back with a thud. Al was 'out to get them'.

'Daft wimp,' said Joe, but the comment was heavy with apprehension because Al was large and belligerent. 'Maybe they'll leave soon.'

'No chance. Mum and Mrs. Bailey will talk about the church jumble sale for hours.'

Joe grimly set aside his work. 'Then we'd better get on with it.'

'That's something really great about you, Joe, you face up to things. Right now I'd rather take to the hills.'

Joe scratched his ear in embarrassment. He had still to face up to the biggest problem of all: would he have to steal for the rest of his life in order to please his dad?

He didn't want to steal. He hated the idea. His stomach heaved when he thought of it.

The answer had been in his mind for days but he had refused to listen. It was time that he did. He would have to find the courage to tell Dad how he felt and face his disappointment. He didn't want to tell him. He hated that idea too.

Either way seemed to lead to the same kind of misery! If this was God's solution, it was a tough one.

They went downstairs. Clive said, 'It's all very well *wanting* to make friends, but that has to work both ways.'

Joe pulled a face. 'Don't remind me.'

The front door stood open to the warm afternoon, and they stepped outside and started down the path.

The car door flew open and Al bolted along the lane. 'Hey!' Clive shouted after him in astonishment.

They raced to the gate, fumbled it open and ran through into the lane. Al was already miles ahead.

'What's going on?' Clive gasped as they ran.

'Don't ask me. I thought *we* were supposed to be scared of *him!*'

'Hey, Al, wait, we want to talk to you,' Clive found the breath to shout.

'*Need* to talk, you mean,' Joe mumbled.

They caught up with Al at the river. He was leaning against a tree trunk, bent over and clutching his sides, dragging in great gulps of breath. 'Stay away,' he managed to say.

Clive and Joe skidded to a halt in front of him. 'Look, Al, what's this? All we want to do is talk.'

'Oh sure! I let you get close to me and you thump me, no thanks!'

Joe's eyebrow rose. So Al was judging them by his own standard. Clive's chest heaved from the run. 'No thumps, just talk. We need to straighten out a few things – '

Al suddenly drew one enormous breath and jumped

into the river. Clive's jaw dropped. Joe blinked.

Al had evidently misjudged his jump because he came to the surface with arms and legs thrashing right in the deepest middle. 'Help!' he shrieked. 'Can't swim!'

'Oh, oh' Clive said in a small voice.

As one Joe and Clive hit the water in a smooth shallow dive and swam toward the frightened boy. Clive reached him first and Al lashed out at him. 'Stay away!' He went under again and Clive dragged him to the surface by his hair.

Joe pulled up alongside. 'Don't be dumb, Al, there's nobody else around to save you. Come on, let Clive swim you back to the bank.' Joe was treading water and was short of breath. 'Clive's done life-saving, trust him.'

Al went under again and this time both boys pulled him up. 'Twit!' Joe screamed at him.

Al seemed to lose interest in escape. He clung to Joe, his eyes big and frightened. Clive cupped his hand under Al's chin and stroked to the bank. They helped him out and all three sat on the river edge, dripping and gasping.

'What made you jump in when you couldn't swim?' Joe ventured presently, genuinely interested in the mental workings of an idiot.

Al wiped his eyes. He looked shame-faced. 'I thought you were out to get me.'

'So you keep saying,' replied Joe wearily. 'We thought you were out to get us.'

'Why would I do that?' Al asked in astonishment.

'It's what we heard.'

'Oh, that,' said Al dismissively. 'What else was I supposed to say when kids kept asking me about the race and how did I feel about losing and all? If I'd kept my mouth shut, no one would've known about that business between you and me, Clive. Or that Joe switched markers.'

'Hmm,' said Clive.

'But I was cross, and I stormed around and pretty

soon kids started asking questions, and it all came out. After that, well, I had to stand up for myself, didn't I?'

'Hmm,' said Joe.

Al said dispiritedly, 'I hate the thought of starting school. They'll find out what happened today and everybody'll laugh at me.'

'We won't tell,' Clive assured him.

'Maybe you wouldn't at that,' said Al thoughtfully. His face fell. 'But they'd hear all the same, bet on it.'

He was probably right. The bush telegraph worked here as well as in Africa. Joe cleared his throat. 'If we all go into school together on the first day and spend every spare minute with each other, that should keep 'em quiet.'

Clive looked at his friend with admiration. Al lifted his head. 'You mean just like all three of us were mates?'

'Exactly like that.'

Clive put in, 'Who knows? It might even get to be a habit. Come on, Al, let's get back and dry off, then you can tell us – '

Joe dug him in the ribs and sent him a warning look. Clive caught on at once. Asking Al about his famous brother was no way to begin a friendship if Al had problems living up to him.

Clive began again. 'Then you can tell us about your last school. Did you like sports?'

Al's eyes lit up. 'Soccer. I liked soccer. Do you play soccer here?'

They went off, arguing amiably about their favourite teams in the first division.

Al and his mother left soon afterwards and the two friends went to sit on the paddock fence and watch Miss Blossom.

'Al's not so bad.'

'Not half. I'll bet he's a good centre forward. He's funny, too, when he talks about playing in his school team.'

They reflected comfortably about the new schoolmate who had promised to come the following day and kick around a soccer ball with them.

Miss Blossom looked at them from across the paddock and returned to grazing.

'Does she really sneer?' asked Joe. 'I mean, horses don't really sneer, do they?'

Clive grinned. 'No, it's just that her mouth isn't formed quite right.'

'Still, it's funny how her mouth curls every time I do something she doesn't like. I reckon she knows exactly what she's doing.'

Clive burst out laughing. 'Maybe you're right.'

Joe took out his pingpong ball and practised rolling it through the fingers of one hand and then the other and talked about a new trick he had in mind.

'You have this box with a girl in it, and then you saw her in half – '

Clive groaned. 'Poor Louisa. She won't take kindly to being stuffed in a box and being sawed in half!'

'Louisa will get used to it.'

'Get used to what?' Louisa enquired, nearing the fence.

'Being part of a magic act.'

'Well, I wouldn't mind. It could be fun. Look what came in the post, my new seed catalogue. And there's a letter for you, Joe.' She climbed up on the fence beside them to study her catalogue.

Joe's letter was from his dad. He opened it and read eagerly.

Mr. O'Brien had been promised a gardening job when he left prison because of his excellent work in the garden, and he was 'pleesed', very 'pleesed', which Joe would easily understand because he knew his liking for plants and such. But, and the word was heavily underscored, he would not take the job unless Joe agreed. After all, the letter went on, they were a 'teem' and he didn't want anything Joe didn't want.

Joe stared down at the badly spelt letter and felt a [illegible]at warmth spread through him. Of course he wanted Dad to take the job! He wanted them both to finish with being the bad guys.

God had turned up trumps! He and his dad could be the good guys after all, and Dad might even go to church with him and like what went on there, the music, the peace and comfort, and hear the good things that Jesus had said. They would be a team again, but this time they would work with God, not against him.

'Good news?' Clive asked.

Joe grinned. 'The best. Just listen to what my dad wrote – '